ARACELY AND OTHER STORIES

Table of Contents

"Whatever happens is what happens." The first time I met Aracely that thought was on my mind, just as we landed in Burbank. I was looking forward to starting law school. Part-time law school, three nights a week. We were in the back of a Southwest Airlines flight from Phoenix. She was in the window seat in the row in front of me, and when we arrived at the gate I overheard her conversation with the couple beside her. As they stood, the man predicted we would be allowed to exit from the nearest door, at the rear, instead of waiting to be the last to disembark, from the front. The woman agreed, but Aracely said she didn't think so. He told her she was mistaken, and made an effort to slip around me. They opened the front door, so he stopped. Aracely smirked. She stood by her seat, scrunched under the overhead bin. Cute girl, but too young for me.

Nevertheless, while we waited, holding our carryons, I felt compelled to speak: "How did you know? Are you psychic?"

She gave me a funny look, and very determinedly responded: "Yes, I'm psychic." It made me laugh, and I wanted her. But of course it was out of the question.

The second time I met Aracely she was walking toward the back entrance of West Valley Law School, a remodeled two-story office building. I was behind her, again, and that high-lighted brown hair motivated me to abandon my plan of going to the front entrance. I caught up with her and pulled open the side door. She smiled and I nodded, as she entered. Of course I hadn't recognized her. Not then.

She appeared to know where she was going. So, being unfamiliar with that section of the building, I followed her. It was the second evening of the semester. She proceeded along the hall to the stairwell. My room was upstairs, too, somewhere. She went up, I went up. She walked down another hallway. I followed. Hearing me, Aracely turned to glance back, smiled almost imperceptibly, and walked on. I had forgotten to smile, being daunted by her look. But those determined eyes seemed mysteriously familiar.

Knowing only the room number, I checked the ones I passed, calculated it was ahead, happily noticed she went into a room toward the front of the building, and even more happily realized, as I approached, that it was my Torts class. Or, rather, our Torts class.

Should I have sat beside her? No way, my nerves told me. Yes way, my gut told me. But I just couldn't. Not yet.

There were a few others inside. Early. Ten minutes early. Aracely sat in the last row, on the aisle. I didn't want to (on principle, anyway) sit in the rear of the classroom. However, I sat in the row in front of her. Couldn't resist. It was a relatively small room--wouldn't be far from the professor--only two rows more. Short tables, each with four chairs on both sides of the aisle.

I put down my bag, took out notepad, pencils, and those heavy books. New books for a new course. The night before I'd had my first class in over two decades: Introduction to Legal Studies. I heard Aracely setting her stuff out, and the thought occurred: what are you doing, dirty old man, she's half your age, and that reminded me of the airplane the week prior, the girl I'd joked with, and of thinking a similar thought. Yeah, you fool, her boyfriend would kick your butt, her parents would be dismayed, she would frown, at the very least, should you ask her out. Forget about it.

A tall student who had been lingering in the hallway as we passed entered, now, sitting in the front row, to the left. He didn't look <u>that</u> young, thank God. Maybe 30 or so.

Finally it hit me: was that the same girl? I had to look, to see. Feigning interest in who else entered, I glanced around at the doorway. A young dark-haired woman entered, speaking with a dark-haired man--both in their twenties. I casually directed my eyes to Aracely. She lifted hers, giving me that impersonal smile once more. I nodded, gave her a comparable smile, looked at her notebook and pens and books, for no reason, and paused, glancing back to her. She wasn't looking at me. But it <u>was</u> her. Couldn't be, but it was.

The third time I met her we were leaving the law school, the next evening, after Contracts. Aracely, carrying her bag of books, was maneuvering through the outside door. I tried to help her, not too successfully, saying: "Here, wait," and she rewarded me with a full smile and a 'thank you.'

"Sure, no problem," I laughed, having only grabbed the door as she was more or less beyond it. But the look on her face encouraged me: "Do you like Professor Henry?"

"I suppose so. Do you?"

We walked toward the parking lot.

"Yes, he's funny."

"It seems so complicated."

"It is. It's going to be difficult."

She held out her hand. "I'm Aracely. You can call me Shelly, if it's a problem for you."

"Are you kidding?" I shook her hand.

"Well, Shelly is easier for people."

"But you prefer Aracely?" Fortunately, I said it correctly.

"Uh-huh." That smile again.

"I'm Ed. You can call me Eddie if it's too difficult for you." Luckily, she laughed.

"But you prefer 'Ed'?"

"Uh-huh."

She stopped at what must have been her Range Rover. I said: "I saw you in Torts."

"Yes! Were you here last semester?"

"No, no. Just starting."

"Oh," she nodded, getting keys from her purse. "You're taking Intro, then?" Off my nod she smiled, again. "Watch out--the professor comes on like your friend, but he grades hard!"

"Thanks for the warning. Didn't you do well?"

"A 'B'. Thought I'd get an 'A'." She opened her door, put in her bag, climbed in. "See you."

I sat in front of her in Torts and Contracts the following week, and the third week the Torts professor separated us into groups, each briefing an 'assault' case. Aracely and I were in the same group, along with the other female students from her row. We broke down an appeals court decision into 'issue-rule-analysis-conclusion.' It was enjoyable; her hair looked good, her lips looked delicious and I contributed far more than I otherwise might have. At one point Aracely remarked favorably on a point I'd made in contradiction to another's. She said it "made sense."

That was a confidence booster. In law school the questions can come fast, and a hard shake of the professor's head in response to an answer can lower your confidence. But you must keep trying.

During the break I was having a cigarette when Aracely stepped out to stand nearby. Normally she remained in her seat, studying.

"Hey, thanks for backing me up in there."

"I thought you were correct. We'll see when he goes through our synopsis!" Ah, that smile. But she kept her distance from the smoke.

Showing off, I said: "Even if 'contact' isn't made, attempted battery is 'assault.' I'm sure he said that last week. 'Placing the other person in <u>apprehension</u> of a battery is enough.'"

"Uh-huh."

I felt like putting her in 'apprehension' of a kiss, but of course, didn't. She said no more, but stayed, so I asked:

"Where are you from? Around here?"

"No, Glendale."

"You drive from there?"

"It really doesn't take that long."

"That's good. I live ten minutes away."

"You're lucky."

I felt lucky. The top strands of her tie-up blouse were open, exposing some skin.

The tall student from the front row approached us, with a paper coffee cup.

"Hi," he said.

"Hello," Aracely said.

"Hello," I was forced to say. He took a sip of his coffee. No one spoke. She looked at him, then at me, and asked: "You haven't had Criminal Law yet?"

She must have known, but I answered: "No, this is my first semester."

"Me too," the other student replied, as though she'd asked him. "Is it very difficult?"

"No, no, it's sort of like this class, only more serious crimes."

"Like murder...and rape?" I was glad I hadn't said that--it didn't go over too well.

She blinked. "Uhh...yes...the more serious crimes, generally. You learn the rule, study past cases, like here, and apply the law to certain fact--uh--fact patterns." She'd stumbled a bit. I wondered why. But he

shouldn't have mentioned murder and rape like that. Idiot.
So I said:

"Yeah--fact patterns. Which rule to apply, did they
do it or not, based on those facts." Just trying to help.

Three women passed by, returning from their cars, I
presumed. The tall guy said, looking at his watch:
"Almost time to go back."

My cigarette was done. I put it out in the stand-up
ashtray. "Let's go."

Aracely turned, the tall guy held the door for her, we
all went in. What was I thinking, anyway, and showing off
for? He was much closer to her age.

The next night, in Contracts, a peculiar thing
happened. As I entered I saw my usual seat was occupied by
someone who had previously sat to the right, in the center
of my row. The chair on the aisle behind him was empty.
Aracely had moved from her usual place, too. So I took it;
now I was beside her. Another reason it seemed strange
was, in addition to the male student (whose name I couldn't
recall) taking my normal spot, and Aracely changing seats,
Professor Henry was strolling around the room marking a

paper. As I settled in, saying Hello to Aracely, he approached, asking me:

"Are you okay here? I'm making up the permanent seating chart."

I shrugged. "Sure." My first thought was: the student in my old place must have felt he wanted the aisle seat 'permanently,' and taken advantage of my not getting there early. The second thought: this is much better, being next to Aracely. And she seemed happy about it, too.

Five minutes into the class I had another thought, recalling how what's-his-name and Aracely had appeared to be friends, from the start, talking a lot before and after each class. Was this arranged between them? Did she want to sit beside me? She'd laughed at a few of my asides, corny as they were. Who knows with women? My ex had complained about my jokes, but loved me, regardless.

The professor put every name on the chart, explaining he was attempting to learn them. Must be hard with a new roomful each semester. He'd refer to his page when anyone raised their hand, and call them by name. I learned the tall guy in front, who answered often, was Victor. But the others' names eluded me. Two were very similar, Armenian and Iranian: 'Her-rash' and 'Ar-rach,' they sounded like.

Two more weeks into the schedule I still hadn't mastered them, and asked Aracely to help me. She did, pronouncing them carefully. I pointed to both, in turn, vainly attempting to distinguish the differences in sound.

"How can you remember them?" I asked her, chuckling. She merely shook her head. "Like, what's <u>her</u> name?" I indicated a woman in the row across from us.

"Ellen!" She had told me already.

"I'm just not good at people's names."

"You have to care about learning them!"

That shut me up.

2

The Torts professor didn't use a seating chart; he didn't care to learn names. Much simpler that way. But I sat next to Aracely, anyway. Why not, after that unusual maneuvering had led me alongside her in Contracts? She readily moved over, giving up the aisle seat.

Aracely was sweet, laughing when I kidded, and complimenting me when I responded with a correct answer. I returned the favor, although she often preferred not to raise her hand even if she knew the answer to one of the professor's many queries.

My Introduction to Legal Studies course was also fun, in spite of her absence because, as she'd informed me, the teacher was warm, friendly, and kind. Naturally I was concerned as per her warning that the exam (or more precisely, his grading) would be tough. Victor was in the front in that class also, talking a lot. He was okay; he wasn't afraid to screw up, which he did on occasion. 'Trespassory breaking-and-entering' he confused with 'trespassing,' and the professor reprimanded him. Gently.

"Those are separate crimes, they are distinctly different words. Lawyers must use words with care. Do you understand the difference in meaning?"

"Yes--I think so. Trespass--"

"When you're before a judge, or a jury, you'll need to be clear in order that they may discern the point you're trying to put across."

"Yes, sir. I meant 'trespassory,' not 'tres--"

"The judge will cut you off and he may not give you an opportunity later to clarify what you <u>meant</u> to say. Understand?" Victor nodded and the professor wandered down the aisle, waving his arm. "In court you'll be <u>talking</u>, just talking. Don't get mixed up. You only need to persuade, to convince." I was writing it in my notes. "But you must use the appropriate words. Now, who can tell me what we mean by these terms: 'trespassory' and 'trespassorily,' in connection with breaking-and-entering?"

I raised my hand as did others. He called on a 40ish woman in the last row, nodding pleasantly to her.

"Uh...'without consent.'"

"Without whose consent?"

"The, uh, owner of the property."

"Almost right. The breaking-and-entering must be accomplished without the consent of <u>whom</u>? The owner?" No one said anything. "Or, rather, the <u>possessor</u> of the dwelling house? Which includes...what? What's included in the definition of 'dwelling house'?" He nodded to a black girl in the front row who always seemed to answer correctly.

"Any structure within the curtilage."

"That's right. It's a distinction we'll cover later, but for now we're only concerned with the definition of the rule. Under Common Law, when must the trespassory breaking-and-entering take place, to constitute a burglary?" He looked at me, no doubt because I'd had my hand up earlier.

"At night." Thank God I'd studied that law before class.

"What about at, say, dusk?"

"Well, yes, if that's after sunset."

"Does dusk occur after sunset?"

"Yes, sir." I hoped that was true. Sometimes when they question you, simple things become elusive. But he was nice to me.

"That's right. Common Law Burglary takes place after sunset--until what time?" The professor looked for another person to answer. Victor had his hand up, naturally, and he nodded at him.

"Sunrise, I believe."

"Yes, 'at night' refers to any time between sunset and sunrise."

Little did I know that within four weeks Aracely and I would be trespassorily breaking-and-entering the dwelling house of another, <u>at night</u>.

3

My friend Jeff called Thursday. To have lunch. I picked him up at his house. Jeff was married, with three children. The family was a good one, his wife was kind and full of energy, the kids were well-behaved. Still, I was glad to be single, and glad my ex had been more interested in building up her real estate office than raising children. Now. At the time I'd wished she would hit that level of success she'd set for herself, and get pregnant. But we'd waited so long the idea lost its allure, and we gradually drifted apart. Not that I didn't still care for her. But that's how it goes sometimes.

Jeff knew her. In fact, he'd introduced us, a million years ago. They'd worked for the same company before she started her own. Now he worked for her. I didn't envy him, no, sir.

"Hey, how's it going?"

"Good, man. I started school."

"Great. Is it alright?"

"Definitely. But hard. You wouldn't believe it. I'll be happy to get passing grades."

"Oh, bullshit."

"Really. It's much harder than college."

I drove us to Johnny Rockets. After we ordered we sat outside so I could smoke. He occasionally did, too, but that day he didn't ask for one. And I didn't push it.

"How's everyone?"

"Great. Fine."

"Sophie not pregnant again?"

"Ha-ha. No. No more for us."

The waitress brought me coffee, him tea. Iced tea, even though it was a little cold out.

I told him about Aracely, how I thought she'd switched seats so she could be next to me.

"The guy in front's her friend?"

"They act like it. He's married, though."

"It could have been arranged. Ask her out. Find out."

"No, no."

"Why not?"

"She's...twenty-four, looks like. I don't know."

"Ask her! What's the harm?"

"You're in bad with me if she says no."

The waitress brought our burgers. I put out my cigarette.

"More coffee?"

"Sure."

"How about you, ready for more iced tea?"

"No, thanks."

"Enjoy, gentlemen."

After she left I said: "Hear what she called us?"

Jeff laughed. "She's extremely credulous."

I did ask Aracely out. It wasn't easy, and it took a week to do it, but I did. And she said yes. The way I framed it, she couldn't say no: coffee at Ruby's before class. Only she rarely drank coffee, so she had water.

Ruby's was a 50's style restaurant near the West Valley campus. They served fantastic shakes, but we both resisted.

"Not hungry?"

"No, thanks," she answered demurely.

"Come on, the burgers are terrific. Or have a salad."

She had a salad. I got a cheeseburger. It felt more like a date that way, only I was unsure how she felt about it.

We briefly discussed the reading assignment, and the standard topic of beginning law students: how distant

graduation day was. And mine was more distant than hers.
But I wanted to ask her something:

"Remember coming into Burbank Airport a month ago?
The back of the airplane?"

Aracely's look was priceless.

"Why, yes, I..."

"They didn't open the rear door, and you absolutely
knew they wouldn't?" Her eyes widened but I didn't let her
speak. "You must have been psychic." That did it.

"Ed! You? That was you!" She laughed so loudly it
drew the attention of other customers. And she reached out
to grab my forearm. "I can't believe it! I remember that.
But, why...?"

"What?"

"Why didn't you say something? You're too funny."
She shook her head, taking a large forkful of salad.

"I don't know. It never felt appropriate."

"You're strange," she said, chewing.

I ate, too, enjoying her reaction.

"I should have known that was you," she commented a
moment later. "Don't keep any more secrets from me. I
hate secrets."

"Alright. I hate them too."

"Do you live in Phoenix?"

"No. I was visiting an old buddy from college. He's a lawyer."

"A lawyer?"

"Yeah. A good guy. Very smart, too."

"Is he shocked at what you're doing?"

"I'll say."

"What did you do? Party?"

"No! Just hung out with his girlfriend, went hiking, had dinner--I was only there two days." When she didn't respond, I said: "And picked up a prostitute."

"You what?"

"Kidding."

"I'm not so sure."

"Really. She was only a stripper."

"Ha! Some strippers are prostitutes."

"How would you know?"

"I don't. But I've heard that."

"If she was she didn't tell me."

"Are you making this up?"

"Yes."

She actually punched me on the arm.

In Torts we struggled over the many circumstances necessary to make an actionable claim, including whether the tort is intentional or negligent. I mangled my notes, didn't volunteer to answer questions. Not only was my mind wandering to our 'date,' I was recalling a real stripper I had met in Washington, DC, in the late nineteen-seventies. Couldn't stop thinking about her, even with Aracely next to me.

The club was the Silver Dollar. Not the fanciest place. There were four or maybe five acts, each different, but one caught my eye more than the others. Beautiful body, a wonderful artistic dance that ended with moving lights on a dark stage, scarcely revealing her nakedness. My friends, however, liked an athletic stripper who set up a display of medals she'd won in the past. She danced around a big board, nearly her height, that was covered with them. I was surprised she hadn't worn them, but with all the flips and jumps she did, I realized why.

Later the owner brought her over to introduce us. I proffered a compliment, naturally, but wanted to meet the other one. Medal-winner sat to talk; my friends bought her a drink and had more themselves. They worked for a lobbyist; all except one, who'd come with me on the trip.

It was spring break and we were flirting with the idea of joining the firm; it was post-Watergate, an exciting time in the nation's capital.

I discreetly asked the owner about the 'shadow' dancer. He took me into the back to meet her. She was radiant, even with clothes on. Asking her for a date was far easier than Aracely. And she wasn't shy about eating a big meal.

We'd ducked out on the others with hardly a word, and made it to an all-night coffee shop. In those days there were lots of them. Patty was her name. Patty had four cats, she said. By the end of our meal she asked if I wanted to see them.

She hadn't asked me for money, and now I regretted not giving her any. I'm sure she could have used it. I'd wanted to call when I returned to Los Angeles, but somehow never did. Another regret.

By the end of Torts I wasn't sure what I'd written, was barely able to recall the subject of the lecture. Have to ask Aracely for her notes, or my grade would drop.

Outside she thanked me a third time, it seemed, for the salad.

"My pleasure. Let's do it again."

"If you want to. I'd like that."

I stopped at a 7-Eleven for smokes and beers and then drove my Camaro to the Blockbuster closest to my apartment. It was still open, so I went in to find a movie to rent. Usually I was worn out after class, and only wanted to sleep. But this lecture had been less intense due to my spending the majority of the time focusing on Patty (and Aracely). That night I felt an urge to stay up.

There was a new Jennifer Lopez movie out, which I grabbed. She reminded me of the stripper: sexy, a little hard, unpredictable, fun.

The newsstand next door was open, too. Naturally. Lefty (he called himself) was working the night shift, as always, wearing a hat to cover his baldness, as always. I bought a newspaper.

"Hello, Edward. How's it going?"

"Breathtaking."

"Don't lie."

"I'm not lying." I lit a cigarette, standing away from the magazine rack in deference to his sporatic flow of business. Lefty grinned.

"Now, Edward, life can't possibly be that good."

"Tonight it is."

"Praise the Lord."

"Did you ever meet someone who struck your fancy?"

"Hundreds of them." A thin man bought a magazine, rolled it up and said solemnly:

"Good night, Lefty. I'll see you tomorrow."

"I mean one out of the hundreds."

"She broke my heart, Edward. She broke my heart."

"They can do that, can't they?"

"You're telling me." Lefty had been a news journalist, at one time, but decided to sell it instead. Much easier, he once told me. Less complicated.

"Well, we'll see how it goes. Long odds."

That brought a laugh. I stepped on my cigarette, threw the remains in the trash. "Gotta go. Hang in there."

"Keep on believing," he replied, pointing to his ever-present Bible near the register.

Aracely had informed me she worked during the day at a place called "OK Skin Care," as receptionist, cashier, and on occasion, janitor. So I visited her. It was a small salon with two hairstylists who also doubled as skin care specialists.

"No, no facial," I said.

"Come on, it's good for you!" She was teasing me as I stood beside her desk, watching the two women work on customers.

"Another time."

"Your hair could use coloring."

My hand went up to what I knew were far too many grey hairs above my ears. "I'll think about it."

"Better not wait too long."

"Is it bad?"

"If you want a young girlfriend it is."

"Who said I wanted a young girlfriend?"

"Nobody. How about a Swedish massage?"

"Now you're talking." I looked toward the back. "Let's go."

"Not by me, silly."

"No?"

"We have trained therapists. Very good."

I snapped my finger in front of my chest. "Oh well. How much?" It wasn't a bad idea.

"Fifty, for an hour." She handed me a tiny brochure. I looked it over.

"Maybe so. Do you--uh, yeah, great--steam room. Maybe so."

In fact, the following week I did have a steam and a massage, but this day we ate lunch in a sandwich shop downstairs, in her building.

"It's a good job. Six days a week. Pays my bills."

"When do you study?"

"I can study up there. And after I get off, when I don't have class." We were both eating turkey sandwiches, mine with coffee, hers with water.

"And on Sundays?"

"I sleep." Oh, how I wanted to ask about her social life, but I controlled myself.

"Not married?" Safe question.

She shook her head, chewing. Her eyes asked me the same.

"Was," I replied. "Twelve years."

"Any children?"

My turn to shake my head, and eat. I didn't want to go into it. She let it go. Then...

"Why do you want to become a lawyer?"

I shrugged. "To help people, and make money."

"In that order?"

It made me chuckle. "Yeah. I've tried it the other way around. What about you? Why do you?"

She gave me that smile. "Same reason."

Next week, after my normal workout of push-ups, sit-ups and treadmill, in my apartment, I went to OK Skin Care for a steam and massage. Aracely showed me the lockers, steam room, showers, and robe. When I was ready a young Asian masseuse led me to her room and left, so I removed the robe, lay face down on the table, put a towel over my butt. In a minute she'd returned.

"How are you?"

"Fine," I replied, thinking: hadn't she just asked me that?

"Good," she said, putting oil on her hands.

The oil was hot, the massage was great. Sometimes they aren't. I told her not too much pressure. When I turned over she discreetly held the towel, looking away. But to my pleasant surprise, when she got around to my midsection, her fingers went under the towel and brushed me, slightly. And again. Finally she tossed the towel aside and massaged my legs with long strokes, making contact with my growing erection each time.

"That's good," I remarked as she did, hoping to encourage her to further exploration. But that didn't work. I knew they weren't <u>supposed</u> to touch you there, but they weren't supposed to remove the towel, either. Finally I said: "You can touch it, don't be afraid."

She laughed, but shook her head. "Not allowed. Sorry."

Of course I didn't tell Aracely what happened, but I determined to return. Perhaps the masseuse was waiting to see if I'd come back for more of the same. And I left her a generous tip. Not that I could afford it. My weekend job at the County Fairgrounds barely managed to pay tuition and fill my refrigerator.

"Whatever happens is what happens." That line was in my mind later, at school. Aracely seemed happy I'd gone to the salon. Contracts was complicated, as usual. Somehow I kept thinking about the massage, and the masseuse. What had she said? Worked there six months, lived in Hollywood, just returned from a weekend in...San Francisco. I hadn't asked her what she'd done up there--too personal. Maybe she'd gone with a customer. Maybe I should ask her to go on a short trip. To Santa Barbara, or...

No, Aracely wouldn't like it. But, so what? Aracely wasn't thinking of me in that way, anyway. Or was she? No, no, no. She must have a boyfriend.

I asked her, too. Why not? After Contracts, on the way to our cars. Yes, she had a boyfriend, from college. Duh. She even showed me his picture. Nice-looking fellow, about her age. They'd graduated together. Sure, I must meet him sometime. No, he doesn't go to West Valley. I didn't ask where he was. Screw it.

That night I turned on the news and had a few beers. Then I turned off the TV, thought about the two girls. Was I crazy? They're both in their early twenties. The masseuse must have a boyfriend too. But I couldn't escape the memory of those fingers rubbing around me, against me, under me, over me, and one time, onto me.

4

An 'offer' can be accepted late if the <u>offeror</u> feels like waiving the time limit. The <u>offeree</u> has to notify the <u>offeror</u> of 'acceptance' or there's no contract. Of course if the <u>offeree</u> begins to perform the duties of the contract (like painting a house, or whatever) in the presence of the <u>offeror</u>, it serves as notification of 'acceptance.' Unless the <u>offeree</u> says it's not necessarily an 'acceptance.' Then it isn't. Yikes. Back and forth it goes. Unless unless unless.

I admired Professor Henry for being able to keep it all straight. I had to take a lot of notes. Aracely typed hers into her laptop, on the table, now, as did many of the students. But I'd only made $200 over the weekend, selling posters and pictures of old cars at my vending stall. Later with that laptop luxury. Much later.

She was oddly quiet. Didn't laugh when I whispered that a contract was like a rat maze. Not that it was very funny, but...she was distant all night, not answering even <u>one</u> of the professor's many questions.

Afterward, outside, I caught up with her and asked: "What's wrong?" half-expecting the reply to be, in some way, about my visit to the salon.

"I'm sorry, Ed. I'm not myself. Genie--you know, your therapist? She's missing."

"What? What do you mean?"

"Missing. Didn't come to work, didn't call. There's no answer on her cell phone. I left messages on both her phones. Lots of them."

"That's unusual for her?"

"Completely. I can't stand it. It's, like, three days. Almost." We arrived at her Range Rover, she fumbled with her keys.

"Maybe she simply took off. Quit."

"Maybe." I helped her open the door.

"Has anyone gone to her place to check?"

"No. I guess I will."

"Sure. Do you know where she lives?" Off her nod I added: "I'll go with you. Don't worry."

"Will you?"

"Of course. Now?"

She hesitated. "It's late..."

"Not that late. Let's go."

"Okay." She looked in her book for the address. "I've got it."

No one answered our knock. Genie had an apartment in old Hollywood: "The Green Palms" it said in the front. Aracely called her cell number again. I looked around the building. About ten units. Dirty place. Trash in the yard. I saw lights on in the apartment next to hers.

"Let's ask them," I said, moving toward the door. Aracely grabbed my arm.

"No. Let's...call the police."

They said to come in and file a missing person report. It took a long time. They did give us coffee. Aracely was distraught, didn't know much about the girl: friends, family, nothing. Couldn't remember any references she'd provided. That information would be at the salon.

The officer wasn't too pleased about it, but agreed to send a car over to Genie's to look around. Naturally he asked had she been behaving uncharacteristically, was she depressed?

"No," Aracely said, with fear in her eyes.

The police questioned the neighbors, who said they hadn't seen her recently, didn't know anything about her other than she was a nice girl. I had to suggest the manager let us in. The police didn't even want to do that. Sure, it was after midnight, but what the heck. Should be the first thing they do, right?

They told us to wait in the front of the building. I thought Aracely was going to cry, but she didn't. It turned out to be a long night.

Two bodies on two separate beds. Genie and a friend, identified the following day. Both had been stabbed repeatedly. There was a story in the paper, not very large. After all, Los Angeles is a big town. Two murdered girls wasn't _that_ sensational. But the fact of ten-plus stab wounds in each did merit local TV coverage. Until no suspects were found. No evidence to lead to any, the homicide detective told us. And no motive. Not robbery-- nothing appeared to have been taken.

Genie had an older sister who worked in a bar on Beverly. No other family in the United States. The other murdered girl, Yung, had worked in the bar, also, and sometimes stayed at Genie's. She had a boyfriend with a good alibi: he'd been in Hawaii the previous week, with witnesses. Genie had no boyfriend, apparently. The boss at OK Skin Care didn't know much, either.

Aracely was a mess for a number of days. Skipped class, but eventually returned. I tried to comfort her and spend time with her. She kept going to work, but said she had a fight with the boss.

"He's a fucking asshole," she said.

"What happened?" We were having lunch at a Mexican restaurant near the salon.

"I'd rather not talk about it."

"Oh, please. Don't hold it inside, it's not good for you."

She sighed. "You want to know? He makes passes at me."

"Passes?"

"<u>Yes</u>. Always. I've gotten used to it. But this time I yelled at him. Because of Genie, you know, because he didn't seem to care."

"About her? Or you?"

"Both. Told me to grow up. To stop thinking about her. Asshole." She drank a little water, poked her enchilada with a fork.

"What did he do?"

"Ed, Ed. What do you think? Just...hit on me, put his arm around me, called me 'sweetheart.'"

I shouldn't have laughed. Oh, how I shouldn't have. Insensitive. "Sorry," I quickly said, as I felt a rush of guilt at the sight of her tears.

"It's demeaning."

"I know. I'm sorry."

"Fuck you too." She was still crying. Maybe it was good for her, a part of me thought. Another part wanted to take her hand, so I did.

Of course she pulled it away, saying "Don't."

I let her be and ate my own enchilada. What else could I do? A minute later she said she was sorry. I told her not to worry about it. She wasn't crying anymore.

"It's healthy for you to cry," I offered.

"I've been crying a lot."

"Not in front of me you haven't."

"So what? Believe me, I've been crying."

The way she said it made me want to laugh, but this time I resisted the impulse.

Before long Aracely was talking about the murders again: "Detective Figari said Yung's family doesn't know anything that will help. Her brother works for the city, has no record. Genie's real name is...oh, I should have written it down. Korean."

I nodded. "They change them a lot, for some reason."

"Yeah." She was eating, at least. Nearly done. "Her parents are here now. Going to have the funeral back home."

Out of the blue she asked, "Can you keep a secret?"

"I hate keeping secrets."

"I do too. Can you, though?"

"I'll try."

That wasn't good enough. "I told the detective this, but it's supposed to be a secret."

"Okay, okay."

"Carl, my boss, has an extra line of work. He takes girls someplace, sometimes. 'Provides' them."

"Huh? He's a pimp?"

"Not exactly. He arranges for a certain 'activity' for men he knows." She drank her water.

"What are you saying?"

"I don't know much about it, but you can't help picking things up. It's like pimping, but for freaks.

He's gotten a few of the massage therapists involved, and other women from other places."

"Go on."

"They've told me. Genie told me."

A busboy took our plates, and poured more coffee into my cup. Then she said:

"Like, they get tied up, or something."

I didn't say anything.

"It's freak stuff. Bondage. Handcuffs. Blindfolds. Everything. And...I told the detective. He's going to investigate it. They're going to follow Carl around, so don't tell anyone."

"Don't worry, I won't tell anyone. Could be dangerous. You'd better be careful."

All she said was "Yeah," as though she didn't care much, at this point. "I think he did it."

"If you think he did it you shouldn't work for him, you should get away from there." We were outside the building, in my car.

"No, I'll be alright. I want to find out more."

"You're not a detective, Aracely. I don't want you to get killed, too. Seriously."

She kissed me right on the mouth. "Me either. But he could slip up, say something incriminating. I want to be there to hear it." There wasn't anything else I could say. Anyway, the kiss had distracted me. She got out and smiled, leaning into the car. "Call me after class."

"When are you coming back?"

Her eyes flickered. "Next week. Really."

"Okay, but I still want you to quit and not mess around with this."

"Somebody has to do it."

Was that a flip joke? I didn't know. She closed the door and proceeded into the building, up the stairs to the salon. I couldn't resist watching the movement under that tight skirt.

5

I called her after class, from my car. The boss

hadn't been in the rest of the day, and that made me happy.

"How do you feel?" I asked her.

"Worried."

"Why?"

"Second thoughts. I was jumpy waiting for him to walk

in any minute."

"See?"

"I know, but...tell me, Ed. You've seen those shows

on Court TV? Investigations of crimes?"

"Yes. Quite a few."

"So, how come there's no evidence from the scene?

Fingerprints, shoe marks, I don't know...How can there be

<u>nothing</u> to go on?"

"Good question. Bad luck, probably. They don't

always leave telltale evidence."

"Where's the murder weapon?"

"He took it. Why leave it?"

"Yeah, I guess so."

"Can you sleep?" I wanted to go over.

"Yes. No. I don't know. Probably."

I laughed. "Want company?"

She paused, but then said: "Ah, no...I have to call Roy, anyway."

"Sure. No problem." I knew who Roy was. The nice-looking guy in the photo.

"Maybe another time. You're sweet to think of it, though." Think of what, I wondered? But I had to make a wisecrack:

"You wouldn't say that if you knew what I was thinking!" I started to regret it until she responded:

"How do you know?"

During the weekend at the fairgrounds I made more money than usual. Good weather, bigger crowds both days. But my back was sore from loading and unloading the boxes of merchandise. And the band they had there wasn't very good.

Aracely called me three times, said Carl was behaving more strangely than usual. No passes, no flirting, no dirty remarks.

She was off Sunday, her normal practice. Could we meet for dinner? Hurt back or no hurt back, I agreed.

This time she met me at the Hamburger Hamlet. I didn't care for the stress in her face. After ordering we sat quietly. I had my usual beer, she had her usual water. Finally Aracely asked:

"Remember you said she'd gone to San Francisco? She told you?"

"Yes, of course."

"Nobody knows about it. I didn't know, and none of the other girls had heard." She waited.

"Let's see," I thought out loud..."she might have gone with Yung. That cop ought to ask her boyfriend--what's his name--Enrique?"

"Sure. He may know. In fact, he may have known and killed them for it. Jealous or something."

"No, he was in Hawaii."

"He could have sneaked back! Flown here, done it, and then returned, nobody knowing."

"Yeah." I drank. "There'd be a record of it."

"Another suggestion for Detective Figari. I'll call him tomorrow."

"He probably checked the airlines for the week. He's not stupid."

"No, he's not. But I'll call him anyway."

"So what's bothering you? Carl?"

Right then the waitress brought our order. After she left I had to ask her again.

"Well, yes. When I talked to him about Genie's trip, to see if he'd been aware of it, he got angry."

"That figures."

"He said I should forget about it. He threatened to fire me if I didn't 'snap out of it.'"

"Jerk. Knowing you, that wasn't the end of it."

She laughed, for a change. "No...I said: 'You're not at all interested in finding out who killed her, are you? You're only interested in yourself.'"

"And?"

"He slapped me."

No words could come out of my mouth. None that I wanted her to hear. She saw my anger, and quickly said:

"Don't--don't do anything. I'm alright. It's good."

"Good?! That son-of-a-bitch, he--"

"No, Ed. Please. It's a good sign. He's desperate. He's losing it."

"I'll say." Again I held my words in.

"Can't you see? Now he might, I don't know, might make a mistake, might--"

"He's made one. It's my turn to talk to this jerk."
Oh, did I want to use a different word, or words. But I
didn't.

"You can't! That's trouble. I know how you feel. I
wanted to strike back myself, believe me."

So I drank my beer, determined to confront him, no
matter what Aracely said. It wasn't logical, it wasn't
smart. She was right, Carl may blow it now, <u>if he's
guilty</u>, and I could scare him off. And I didn't want to
deceive her. So I said:

"Only to talk to him. Just inform him he's not to go
around slapping you, or anyone else."

"<u>No</u>, please."

"How big is he, anyway?" I asked with a smile. It
worked, she had to laugh a little.

Okay, I thought, I told her, I'm not deceiving her.
And I'll try not to antagonize him.

We ate, we discussed other things. I said I'd give
her copies of my notes from the classes she'd missed. She
told me: "No, thanks, I've seen your handwriting. Dora
can loan me hers. She's been in class, hasn't she?"

"Which one is Dora?"

And again she laughed. "In front of us, next to Haratch!"

I let Monday pass, because I was too mad at Carl to be at all civilized, seeing him. I got through Intro, relaxed in my apartment, exercised, showered, and went to bed, planning what to say to him. If there was a fight, so be it.

The next day I studied a couple of hours and drove to OK Skin Care without calling first. Surprise is always the best if there's going to be resistance. Upstairs they were very busy, with people waiting, the hairdryers in use, the chairs full, the manicurist working. Aracely was on the phone and one woman was waiting at the cash register. Murder publicity makes for good business?

I'd decided to trick her a little, saying I was up for a steam and massage, although the idea felt creepy. Wherever Carl's office was, I figured I could find it.

She got off the phone, the woman paid, and I said: "Hi. Pretty busy."

Aracely could be even smarter than I thought. Her eyes burned into me, she shook her head, she didn't smile--

not even that slight one she occasionally confers on people.

"What are you doing here?"

"Oh, I--"

"And don't say you want a massage."

"Alright, I won't."

She consulted a notebook. "You'd have to make an appointment, anyway. There's only one therapist working, and she's--"

"I know, she's <u>busy</u>. Never mind. You know what I'm doing here. Where's his office?"

Of all things, she gave me that little smile and picked up the phone, pushed a button, waited a second, and said:

"Can you see a customer with a complaint? Fine." She hung up. "He's coming out. Good luck."

Carl came out. Not very big, older than I'd expected. Way more grey hair than me. Stooping shoulders.

"This is Mr. Donahue."

"Hello," I said, controlling my anger. "Can we talk in private?"

Carl Donahue graciously consented; we went to his office. On the way he asked: "Is this about that little trouble at Ho-Ho's?"

"Ho-Ho's?"

"You're not a bartender?"

"No."

"Well, sir, what's the problem?" he asked, sitting behind a small desk. The door was now closed, I still wanted to take a swing at him, but...did he have to call me 'sir'?

"Aracely is a friend of mine."

"Oh?"

"She told me an interesting story."

"Really?" He leaned forward, his hand under the desk. "What was that?"

Not wishing to get shot, I merely said: "It's okay, it's all over. But I'd like your assurance--"

"What's all over?" He leaned back, his hand empty. "What's this 'interesting story'?" Pushy little bastard. But I was relieved not to see a gun.

"I'd merely appreciate your assurance that you won't slap her around again."

Before he could respond his door opened and I saw a muscular Samoan-looking gent enter. Carl waved him to stop.

"Did she tell you I slapped her?"

"Uh, yeah." I moved a step to the side, keeping out of the other guy's immediate reach.

"And you didn't like it?" Dumb question.

"Certainly not."

"So?"

"So? You shouldn't be slapping women, that's all."

"That's all?" He smiled at the big guy. "Suppose she deserved it?"

"That's a stupid remark." I looked at the guy with the muscles. "You the bodyguard?" He didn't say anything, so I took another step to the side.

"Who are you?" Carl asked me.

"A friend of Aracely's, I told you."

"Sorry you came in here now?" He grinned like a maniac. "Get rid of him."

Muscle guy reached with both hands, but I jumped backwards and threw a punch.

He elbowed it away and lunged at me, so I ducked and tried a punch to the belly. A lot of good it did. His hands on me, his knee in my face, an exclamation from Carl, and a hard object struck the top of my head. That's about it, until I woke up in the alley behind the building, glad to be alive. Aracely was there, the sweetest face in the whole world. And she kissed me. Maybe it was all worth it.

"Ed, tell me you're okay."

"I'm okay. Ouch." My head wasn't okay.

"Really! Are you alright?"

"I'm alright. I'm not bleeding?"

She checked, I checked. I stood up.

"Who--?"

"Carl's sorry. Don't call the police."

"The police? No, I--"

"He apologized to me, he doesn't want the police involved."

I looked up the back staircase to a door at the top, wondering how I got out here.

"Where is he?"

"No, Ed. No." More tears. I hate that.

"Look, what's the idea? His bodyguard beats me up, and you say 'no'?" Now she hugged me. It _was_ worth it.

Three aspirin and I got through class that night. Aracely sat beside me, typing. My hand was, sadly, not working very well. A bit shaky. Even I could barely read my notes.

During the break she summed it up for me:

"Tomorrow I'll call Detective Figari to see if he's found out anything. My guess is they're letting it go. Carl has an alibi, and the--"

"Alibi. Who gives a shit?"

"The police do! And they're checking on Enrique-- about the trip to San Francisco. If we say any more Carl will escape, I know it."

"So...you're planning on...what?"

"Just an idea. How's your head?"

"Not bad. Who's that tough guy who hit me?"

"You're the tough guy. Did I thank you for...?"

"No, but why should you? Didn't do any good."

"Yes, yes, it did. Carl's leaving me alone. We've got him right where we want him!"

I laughed. "Funny. What's your idea, may I ask?"

"You may." Aracely took a deep breath. "There's a place he has in Ventura. He asked me to go there several times. Must be a ranch, or a--"

"How many times did you go? Just kidding." Her look was downright mean.

"I <u>never</u> went there. But the manicurist did. She told me all about it. Anyway, I want us to go snoop around." She just looked at me, waiting.

Two choices: tell her she's crazy, or say 'yes.'

I slid in between: "Are you out of your mind? Let the police do it. No, I know, they won't. But it's dangerous. He could be there."

She smiled a full one. "I knew you'd agree! He only goes there on the weekend, so let's do it tonight. If you're up to it."

"I'm not up to it. Sorry, Aracely. This is kind of foolhardy. We should be--"

"Then when?"

"Oh, boy. After we talk to the detective. I want my head clear. Tomorrow night."

Figari knew very little. I spoke to him myself, over the phone. Yung's boyfriend didn't know about any trip to San Francisco, and following Carl had turned up nothing.

"Did you examine Enrique for bite marks?"

"Bite marks? No."

"I've heard you can match them. Maybe one of the girls bit him. They must have put up a fight."

"You see that on Court TV?"

After class we met by her car. But I insisted on driving. I brought a flashlight and a tire iron. You never know. She had water, snacks, and determination. We drove north on the 101. Actually it's west, due to the coastline curvature. She consulted a map on the way.

"Get that from his office?" She was reading a piece of paper with the address. After she nodded I remarked: "Brave girl." Then I remembered the bodyguard. "No bull-necked bruisers around?" She laughed at that, although I hadn't meant it as a joke.

Ventura's an hour, just about, from L.A. Less if you leave from the Valley, which we did. I was more nervous than I should have been. What could happen? Aside from dogs and armed guards, that is. Aracely didn't say much until she began to give me directions.

We found it. Big house in the hills. Three stories, wood and brick, old oak tree in the front. Where did he get his money? I parked a long winding block away. If I'd had any hope she would chicken out at the last minute it evaporated with the sight of her quick advance to the property. There was no fence, no gate. Not in Ventura. No lights, no noise. I held the flashlight in one hand, the tire iron under my coat. She hadn't objected to it.

"Well, should we try to peek in the windows?" Another time, another place, her question might have been humorous.

"No. Let's crunch a few leaves to find out if there's a watch dog."

"Uh-uh. If somebody is inside they'll hear it." She walked onto the front yard. I caught up to her, carefully. She was right, of course.

The nearest house nearby was a safe distance, although it had a porch light. I turned on _my_ light, put my fingers over it, pointed it at the ground. We avoided the front walkway.

My mouth was dry; I didn't know about hers. She was breathing deeply. Just before we got to the house I caught her arm, stepped forward and turned off the flashlight. We looked in a window. Curtained. We made our way to another. Curtained. There was a small window in the front door. I touched her shoulder to indicate she should wait, and ascended the three or four steps to look in. No curtains, but totally dark. Nothing. I returned, shaking my head. We froze when a car drove by, its lights illuminating her face momentarily. The car continued. We were in the shadows, anyway, and the main section of town, although lit up, was far below.

"Let's go around." Her voice was husky.

"Okay." So was mine.

In the back we could see through to an empty kitchen, then through another window to a dining room. There was a small fixture in a wall plug which provided a glowing light. I could see another room through a doorway, partially. She tugged at my sleeve, and pointed to the doorknob of the back door. I shook my head. She accepted it, fortunately, but pulled me toward a garage separate from the house. I had to use the flashlight again, covering it again with my hand, letting out a few slivers of light to help us along.

The garage was large, and Aracely, without asking this time, reached for the side door and turned the knob. It opened.

She looked in but I put my arm in front of her and pointed the light inside. There was a car, a Jaguar, and a bunch of boxes. She pushed at me to enter. Well, it was too late to worry now.

Inside there was an assortment of tools and junk, and another door behind the car. It was locked, but to my surprise, Aracely pulled a key from her coat pocket, inserted it, and opened the door. All I could whisper was: "Careful," and attempt to get in front of her. She beat me to it.

One slow sweep with my light and I was ready to leave. The place was like a lounge, with overstuffed chairs and a bar, and to the rear, a huge bed, all made up. Aracely beckoned me as she made her way to the bed. First she felt it, then smiled at me, and suddenly with a serious look held my flashlight hand, pointing it toward a tall cabinet. Of course she had to open it. Full of what we'd expected: whips, masks, handcuffs, rope, other sex paraphernalia. Bottles of liquid. Lingerie.

I didn't look at it all; I grabbed her and yanked her away, whispering:

"Most definitely time to go, honey."

During the return drive to the Valley she explained the key was a duplicate she'd made from one in his drawer, in the office. I tactfully remarked that we were lawbreakers who attended law school--a bad mix. "But, it's one way to learn."

No laugh. She said, "If Genie and Yung were into that freak stuff with him, getting paid for it, they might have gotten cold feet and he didn't like it."

"The bodyguard could have stabbed them."

"Would they let him in the apartment?"

"Right. Carl was either with him or alone."

"Or it could have been a...'client.'"

"Yeah, could've been. By the way, who's 'Ho-Ho'?"

She stared at me. "What did you say?"

"Who's 'Ho-Ho.'"

"That's what I thought. Don't know anyone by that name."

"'This about the trouble at Ho-Ho's?' That's what Carl asked me. Oh, then he asked if I was a bartender, I think."

"It's a bar. Has to be. Never heard of it."

"I'll call information." We rode in silence.

"Well, partner, we survived it," she sighed, placing her arm around my shoulders.

"Yeah. So far."

At my car outside the empty school I suggested we eat something besides the snacks we'd had on the way, but she declined, yawning.

"I'll follow you home."

"Too far," she responded.

"No, it isn't. I'd rather."

"Really?"

"Unless you want to stay with me tonight."

"I wonder which is safer." My turn to laugh. But she had to add: "Roy wouldn't like it."

"Forgot about him. Okay, I'll follow you."

It was kind of far to her apartment in Glendale, and it was very late. At her door she thanked me profusely for 'everything.'

"Lunch tomorrow?"

She frowned. "Don't want him to get too suspicious."

"True. I'll call you." We hugged. No kiss; it didn't seem appropriate.

6

No 'Ho-Ho's' in Los Angeles or Ventura, so I tried San Francisco. Pay dirt. Gruff guy answered.

"Hello," I said. "Uh, what do you serve there?"

"Just about everything. What do you want?"

"Pacifico."

"Got it."

"Good. What street you on?"

"Geary. Need the address?"

"No, I'll find it. Thanks."

Some detective, too nervous to get the address. Oh well, I was a beginner.

Aracely thought I'd done wonderfully, and told me the boss wasn't in yet.

"Still don't want to have lunch?"

"No," she said. "It can't be good if we're always together. I mean, from his perspective."

"Right. Say, do you have a picture of Genie? A snapshot or--"

"I don't believe so. Wait--she did give me one. Posing in front of 'The Green Palms.' A couple of them. But not the other girl. Why?"

"It's my turn to have an idea."

"What?"

"Go to Ho-Ho's, show it to the bartender."

She didn't say anything. Then: "Very good."

"You approve?"

"Uh-huh. Except there was--"

"Some 'trouble.' I know."

"Trouble Carl heard about," she added.

"So?"

"Nothing. We're in deep, that's all."

"Not too deep," I offered.

"Pretty fucking deep."

She brought me the photo after work. I showed her my apartment, including the bedroom. It didn't seem to impress her.

"Don't you have a girl, Ed?" We sat in the living room.

"Not now. I don't really want one. It's difficult to explain."

"<u>Try</u>. Oh, I get it. You still love your ex-wife!"

"That's not it. Sure, I still love her, but that's not it."

"What, then?"

"Can't find the right one." Aracely looked skeptical.
"I dated my dental hygienist for awhile." She laughed.
"No, really. Nice girl."

"But?"

"Oh, I don't know. She was looking for a husband."

"Anyone else? Must have been others."

"Someone I met at the fairgrounds. Too old for me."
Off her look I said: "My age."

"Ha! That's ridiculous."

"Yeah. Just kidding."

"I think not," she said.

"Listen, you want coffee, or water, or--"

"No, thank you. Have to get home and study."

"Want to study here, together?"

"Sometime, sure. But I'm so tired. Aren't you?"

"I slept in. Didn't have to work, like you."

"Can I ask you something?"

"Of course."

"Can you live on what you make? How do you afford
West Valley?"

"Oh, I saved up some. I used to work for a book publisher. You know, reading all the submissions, making recommendations. I majored in English Lit. At Cal State."

"When did you decide to become a lawyer?"

"I just don't know the answer to that. Everyone asks that." She nodded. "Didn't know what else to do, wanted to meet some cute girls."

She laughed. "Well, I admire you."

"For what, going to law school?"

"Yes."

"You're sweet."

On that she gave me her big smile and stood up, looking for her purse. I got up too, feeling awkward. Outside I kissed her on the cheek, and she held me a long time, saying softly:

"Take care of yourself, and bring back some good information."

San Francisco was a short flight from Burbank Airport. I sat in the back, in memory of the first time I saw that magnificent, expressive face (and body). Have to ask her what she'd been doing in Phoenix that time.

I got a cup of coffee and thought about the situation. Two suspects, at least. Carl, the most likely, or by extension, his bodyguard. Enrique. Or...? No forced entry, no broken windows. No DNA, no foreign fingerprints, no unaccountable items of clothing. Could have been someone who knew Genie, or, for that matter, someone else who knew Yung. Didn't Genie have an ex-boyfriend? That doesn't narrow it down much, Eddie.

I was going to find out something at Ho-Ho's; I felt it. A piece of the puzzle. Something the homicide department could use. Then they can question Carl about that 'trouble' he spoke of. Could be connected to the scene at his home in Ventura.

Then I got nervous. Ho-Ho's could be a link to weird sex traffic, or whatever. Have to watch my butt.

We landed, I rented a car. I drove downtown to Geary Street, immediately realized I needed a phonebook--too long a street to cruise, hoping to spot the bar. Amateurish, but it worked. Finding a phone booth with a book was the toughest part. And parking.

Not a bad looking spot--sort of a neighborhood bar. Inside it was cozy, with fight pictures on the walls. Only

two customers, one bartender. I had the photo in my
jacket.

"Hey," I said nonchalantly, as I sat.

"How's it going?" the husky, Italian-looking bartender
asked. But he didn't strike me as dangerous.

"Let me have a Pacifico." He pulled one out, popped
it open, set it, with a coaster, on the bar. "And a mug,
or a glass, please." He nodded and pulled me down one.
The two men were talking, but not to each other. The
bartender stepped over to them and said:

"Hold it," and laughed. "One at a time." The first
one spoke:

"I didn't put it together until Cecil told me the next
day. A transvestite!"

"Oh, shit," the other man said. "She is not. I know
the lady. Don't you know her?" He was asking the
bartender, who nodded.

"Sure, I know her. She's no transvestite."

The first man raised his voice. "Is too! Bobby would
know, shit, he took her home. I mean, took <u>him</u> home." He
cackled, picking up his glass.

"But Cecil could be bullshitting. Talk to Bobby directly." Again the second man deferred to the bartender. "Right?"

"Right," he said, and glanced at me. I shrugged and took a long sip. The first man gestured to his drink and was poured another.

The three of them continued in conversation until I waved the bartender over.

"Excuse me," I said. "Has this place been around a long time?"

"Twenty-five, twenty-six years. Yeah, twenty-six. My father started it with a buddy of his."

"Oh, really?" I took another sip and he poured the last of the beer into my glass.

"One more?"

"Sure."

After he set it down he indicated, with his thumb, a large photo behind the bar. "That's him," turning and pointing to one of the boxers. "Heavyweight."

I know I should have asked him more, like 'What's his name?' and 'Who did he fight?' but my nervousness and impatience won out. I only said: "Oh, really?" and removed Genie's picture from inside my jacket. But I had the presence of mind to ask: "What's your name, by the way?"

"Hal."

"I'm Eddie." We shook. "Listen, maybe a month or so back this friend of mine came in, I think. Here she is." I showed Hal the photo, and he examined it.

"Can't say I recall her." Of course, he'd have to say that. Doesn't know me from Ted Bundy.

"She might have come in with an older guy, grey hair, stooped shoulders." Hal looked at me. I laughed easily. "No, really, she's a friend. I'm trying to find her. She didn't come back to L.A."

One of the other customers was talking to Hal from down the bar. Hal looked at him, but turned his gaze on me again.

"She's gone missing?" He looked at the photo, then handed it to me.

"Glad to pay you for any information."

"No, no," he chuckled. "That's not necessary." But he didn't repeat the earlier denial--only waited for me to continue.

"This is pretty important. She works for my girlfriend, at a hair salon." I was in deep now. Still

Hal waited. No ideas came to me, so I took a drink. "OK Skin Care," I finally said, and his expression changed just enough to indicate recognition. "The owner's name is Donahue." Either I get shot, or I win.

At last Hal spoke. "Wasn't him. She was with a way younger guy. In his twenties."

I thought: how does he know the 'older' guy is Donahue? At that moment the first man needed a refill. Hal obliged, and poured another drink for the second man. I tried to think fast, but wasn't getting anywhere. The bartender must have done the same, because he returned and said, friendly-like:

"This girl was real nice, but the guy with her wasn't so nice. Can't recall his name, but I do remember throwing him out. That help?"

Was he mocking me, or being straight? No way to tell.

"Drunk?"

Hal merely nodded.

"Spanish-looking dude?" I should have said 'Latin,' but I was nervous.

"Very much so. Know him?"

"Yeah, Enrique." Boy, was I in deep.

His eyes tightened up. Could be he knew the name, had known all along. But now what? The other guys were listening.

"They leave together?"

"They did. Anyway, she followed him out and didn't come back."

"Did he seem angry at her?"

Hal didn't want to answer, only shrugged. To me that meant 'yes.' He wouldn't be afraid to say 'no.' And I had an instinct the trouble Carl referred to was more than this. But what?

"He didn't come back?" The tension was thick.

Hal said, "Not him."

"Someone else?" It was a shot in the dark, but the way he answered gave me the idea.

Now Hal smiled. "Whose side you on, Eddie?"

"Her side." He tossed the empty bottle in the trash, put up a fresh one. A new customer entered. Hal went over to him, took his order. While they talked I thought: if he's on _their_ side, I'm in trouble. I wanted to leave.

When he casually returned to my part of the bar he asked me: "You're on her side?"

"Well, yeah. I'm just looking for her."

"You know Donahue?"

"Slightly."

"You know a big Samoan works for him?"

"Yes."

He paused, then asked gruffly: "They send you up here?"

"Shit, no." I added, "I'm on my own." He laughed, and leaned forward.

"Tell you what, Eddie. You seem like a nice person. How do you like the Samoan?"

"I don't care much for him." Then I got it: "He's the one came in here after you threw Enrique out?" Hal just nodded. "What happened, may I ask?"

He smiled. "You actually don't know, do you?"

"No."

"Well, I'll tell you. He wasn't happy about Enrique's loose tooth."

"Loose tooth?"

"You don't know shit, do you?"

"Guess I don't."

"Came in a week later, tried to scare me. I was having a little sandwich over there." He pointed to a table near the door. "Big fella. Said I shouldn't have

pushed this punk around. Said Enrique's boss didn't like
it. Said I was in need of a lesson. I put my sandwich
down, got up, and gave <u>him</u> a lesson."

When I smiled at that, he chuckled: "My old man
showed me a few punches, over the years."

7

What did that mean--Enrique worked for Carl? One
thing it meant, Carl sent the big dude to hassle Hal. Ha!
He got what he deserved. Didn't know who he was messing
with. Should have known not to mess with an Italian.

I returned to Burbank with so much information for
Aracely my brain was overflowing. After taking the shuttle
to the parking lot, driving to the West Valley, going
through Del Taco, I still couldn't figure it all out.

Friday night. What's she up to? Or up _for_? Called
her cell phone.

"Went well."

"Tell me."

"Where are you?"

"My apartment, but I only have five minutes to talk
now. Roy's picking me up."

When I groaned she snapped at me.

"Knock it off! We're going to dinner. Don't be
jealous."

"What makes you think I'm jealous?"

"That's a laugh. We women know. Just tell me what
happened, quick." Then she added: "Please."

I told her.

"You did great! I'll make it up to you. I'll call you tomorrow. Sorry, but I have to go."

"Okay. Talk to you tomorrow."

Make it up to me? Something else to figure out. But she was right--I was jealous. I smoked about a half a pack of cigarettes and drank more beer. It was cold out so I left the heater on all night. Had a crazy dream about dogs and guns.

In the morning I checked my pistol in the drawer in the bedroom. Loaded. I regretted not going to the practice range for...how many years? I was tempted to carry it with me but that was illegal. Unless I kept it unloaded in the car. Lot of good that would do.

At work the cold weather thinned out the crowds. But we sold a bunch of sweatshirts.

"Why can't the cops pick up this bodyguard? What's his name, anyway?" Aracely had called me at noon.

"Miko," she said.

"Fantastic."

"What?"

"Just sounds weird."

"Racist."

"No, I don't mean it that way. What's the matter?"

"Nothing's the matter, Ed. I'm tired."

"Up late?"

"Wouldn't you like to know."

"Anyway, Figari should talk to him."

"Probably has already," she countered.

"I want to tell him, to make sure. This Miko is bad. Has he ever bothered you?"

"No, not really. He stays in a room behind the showers, waiting. And goes wherever Carl goes."

"Is there a buzzer under his desk?"

"You mean Carl's desk?"

"Uh-huh."

"Yes."

"I thought so. He reached under there and I got hit on the head."

"Look, I'm sorry. But I did tell you not to go--"

"It's not your fault. What's wrong? Did something happen?"

"No. I'm sorry. This is stressful."

"Sure it is." When she didn't respond, I asked: "Want to give it up?"

"No way."

Neither of us spoke for half a minute. I just walked around in a circle. Then I said:

"Come on, let's have dinner. I'll pick you up and we'll--"

"I want you to come over."

"You want me to come over?"

"I'll cook. Okay? Come over."

After six I packed the merchandise away, counted up with my partner, locked the booth, rushed to get a shower and a shave, let Aracely know I was on the way, and bought some flowers. Why not?

To my surprise she was wearing a robe. When she let me in she thanked me for the flowers and said:

"If you don't mind, I don't feel like dressing. Too tired, frankly."

"I don't mind."

Her hair looked beautiful, her face looked fresh and scrubbed, the food smelled good, the music was low. I was in heaven.

She took my jacket, almost pulling it off. We sat in her very tiny living room drinking white wine and relaxing.

At least I was relaxed. She kept getting up and going to the kitchen.

"Please don't expect anything elaborate. It's only pasta and meat sauce. And veggies."

"Terrific."

Her phone rang. Whoever it was didn't get much of her time. And I heard her lie.

"I'm alone, if it's any of your business. All I want to do is have a bite to eat and go to bed."

Aracely had at least four glasses of wine, one during dinner. We ate from her coffee table. Like me, no dining room. But good china.

"Tastes wonderful."

"You like it?"

The dessert wasn't so good (whatever it was) (kind of a cake, but not really).

"Here, let me have that." She took the plate to the kitchen. I didn't object.

"Sorry, I'm too full," I said when she sat down again.

"That's okay. My sister makes that junk and keeps bringing it over. It's called 'Tres Leches.'" Off my look she laughed and said: "You can smoke. I don't care," pointing to an ashtray.

"Truly?"

"Truly."

So I did, wondering if she was wearing undies. I'd had three glassfuls of wine myself.

"Hey, what were you doing in Phoenix?"

She puzzled that for a second and smiled. "Not Phoenix. I'd been in San Antonio. Just changed planes there."

"Lucky for me," I said. Sure, that was pushing it, but it was true.

"We'd have met in class." Always the pragmatist.

I put out my cigarette. "I'm glad it happened, Aracely, because when I recognized you at school I felt more comfortable introducing myself."

"You did? What did you think?"

"What did I think? I don't know."

"Out with it."

"So, why were you in San Antonio?"

"Don't do that. Tell me. Oh, stop. Would you like some coffee?"

"No, unless you do."

"I need it."

"Okay."

She went to prepare it. I could have followed her, but then she'd repeat the question, and what was I going to answer? That I'd thought she was lovely and wanted to sleep with her, and regretted being so much older? Couldn't say that.

Aracely became more alert after she had a cupful, but didn't repeat her question. "More?" she asked.

"No, thanks. Go ahead."

She smiled and returned to the kitchen. I heard her cleaning dishes, but she came out before I got halfway there.

"What are you doing? Oh no. I'll finish them in the morning." She put her hands on my arms, pushing. But instead of backing up I reached my hands around her, pulled her toward me, and kissed her. She struggled free, to my disappointment.

"I have to pee!" Nice.

She left and returned, sitting on the couch beside me.

"Now," she sighed, and leaned forward.

I kissed her, tasting mouthwash, pushing her onto the cushions, rubbing my hands along that soft neck, and robe, noticing the passion in her movements. She put her hands in my hair. I stopped the kiss and readjusted us on the couch lengthwise.

"Take this off," she said, grabbing at my tie. I sat up and did as requested, realizing I had to pee, too. It's not something you can contain for long, no matter how much you may want to. I kissed her once and stood up. She looked at me in the funniest way.

"My turn. Sorry." I went to the bathroom while she laughed.

When I came out she was on her bed. I walked to it slowly, thinking: is this for real? When she pulled at my belt the way she had at my tie, I knew the answer.

8

It was late--after three--when I left. She'd wanted
me to stay, which I nearly did, if it hadn't been for the
dude in the photograph. Aracely read my mind.

"It's over with him," she said at the door.

"What?"

"We had a bad fight--Friday night. It's over."

Not that I was sorry. "In addition to being psychic
you can read minds, too?"

"Yours I can." We shared a good kiss.

Too old for her, dummy. Wake up. She needs a young
man. She's only caught up in this crime, she's wrapped up
in it with you, she's in need of comfort. Well, you
comforted her. Hope the neighbors didn't hear.

I stopped at Winchell's for a donut and a cup of real
coffee. Had to go outside to smoke. Cold, not much
traffic--early Sunday morning. Should quit, anyway. Don't
want to get emphysema.

Did Enrique do it? Crazy, mad at the girls about
something? Had Yung been in San Francisco? What was he

doing up there with them anyway? Bondage 'job'? Carl sent them, sure. But...

Why kill them? Oh yeah: they both must have wanted to get out of the business, and Carl wouldn't let them. What a rotten son-of-a-bitch. I decided to carry my gun in the car, loaded. Then I decided not to. Could get pulled over, busted, and put in jail. Then I thought of Carl, and decided to anyway. Not to mention Miko.

At my apartment I set the alarm and went to bed, thinking of Aracely.

Work was a drag; my partner Robert had a bug up his ass about the fact that I was late, and once more the band didn't sound very good. Nevertheless I had Aracely's mouth and body and vocal responses to occupy me. There was little cadence to her responses; all spontaneous. I got the impression Roy hadn't done much for her lately. Or was that wishful thinking?

She said her mother came from Honduras. They still had relatives there, and had visited over the years, but Aracely was glad she'd been born in the U.S. and preferred to live here. Her folks lived in San Antonio--that's where she'd been before I first saw her, first spoke to her. They were helping her get through law school.

During my lunch break I called, but she didn't answer. I tried her other number; no response. Left an inarticulate message, unsure what our relationship was, now. Then I worried, considering her proximity to danger.

She could be kidnapped, taken hostage, even killed. Robert noticed my mood, thought I was hung over. I let him think it. I liked Robert, but didn't feel at ease discussing the homicides and our investigation into them. Early on, when I had mentioned it, he told me flatly how stupid I was to get involved. So much for that.

But she called; she was alive.

"How's it going? Working hard?" Her voice was subdued, almost, as they say, purring.

"Hardly working."

"Umm."

"Get my messages?" That's better than demanding to know where she'd been.

"Yes. I was sleeping."

"Tired?"

"Not now! I haven't been sleeping very well." That was good for my ego, but I let it drop.

"Thanks for dinner, incidentally."

"That all?"

"Well, you know, everything."

"Everything?" She was playing with me.

"Yes, everything."

"Me, too," she said, quietly.

"Are you going to study?" Had to change the subject. She laughed, noticing it.

"I guess so. I'm behind in the reading."

"So am I."

"Too tired to come over again?"

"Never too tired for you," I answered. But, was that a commitment? Too late to take it back if it was.

"Umm. Good."

We studied, we ate Mexican food I'd picked up on the way. She was yawning by ten o'clock, as I turned on the TV to see the news. I was yawning too.

"What do you think, should I go or should I stay?"

"Stay, if you like."

Tired as we were, it was nearly as good as the night before. Sweetest girl I'd ever known, without a doubt.

In the morning she taunted me for having brought a toothbrush: "So sure of yourself!"

I chased her into the living room, caught her, held her, kissed her. She bit my neck. "Oh no," I kidded, "You have to go to work."

She pulled at my hair. "Come in and get it colored! Or at least cut."

Of course I couldn't do that; Carl and Miko would be there.

9

The police didn't care in the least about Carl's weird sex room. Aracely told the detective she'd 'heard' about it at work, that money was paid for kinky services. The following day Figari said he'd spoken to a vice squad sergeant who didn't care to pursue it. Carl had an alibi, remember?

We remembered, but didn't attach much significance to it. Not as much as Figari did. The 'slap' Aracely described provoked interest, but since she declined to make the complaint official, the police wouldn't pursue that, either. The detective did venture out to question Miko, who claimed innocence, supported by his <u>own</u> alibi. Where did they get them? I didn't even have one.

School wasn't much fun that week. But we studied, we attended classes, we met on Thursday to reconnoiter. Friday night I took her to a movie, a comedy. It helped a little. We spent the night at my place, having slept apart since Monday. Lucky for me she didn't insist on every night. I didn't want to say it, but that would be too much for me.

Saturday night I begged off, too tired from work. And my back was sore. She didn't mind; she was tired from work, too.

Sunday she came to the fairgrounds to see what it was like. Robert was gracious, even a bit smitten. Aracely was her friendly self, and I was only a little jealous. She helped us with the customers, speaking Spanish with more than a few. I watched her sit in the front of the bandstand, evidently enjoying the music. When she returned to our stall, her face was lit up with an idea.

"Ed, Ed, we have to question Enrique ourselves! What he must know!"

It was impossible to resist her energy. "Alright, but how do we find him? Figari won't tell us, that's for sure."

"Fuck him!" Robert's head almost snapped off. He was at the cash register, close enough to hear. "The sister-- she'll tell us. We'll make up a story. Figari knows where she works."

"He <u>might</u> tell you that."

"Fuck him! I'll get it out of him. What's he done, anyway? Nothing!" Robert stared, and I laughed.

She called Figari on Monday, playing it as if she just wanted an update. Naturally he couldn't give her specifics, only generalities. Evidence must be protected. Not an issue, in this case, as there was very little evidence to protect. And he liked Aracely—who didn't?

We met for lunch below the salon.

"He wouldn't tell me the name of the bar, at first, but I reminded him he'd already divulged the street—Beverly Boulevard."

"'Divulged?' You're really talking like a lawyer now. I'll have to correct Robert's first impression of you."

"I wish you would. Doesn't he like me?"

"Oh, sure he does. In fact, your language turned him on."

"Really. What about you?"

"What did Figari say?"

"Answer my question."

"I'm not on the stand."

"Coward," she laughed.

"Objection, Your Honor."

"On what grounds?"

"Nastiness."

"Overruled."

Finally she told me: 'The Road Home.'

"Dumb name for a bar," I remarked.

"Yeah, <u>much</u> dumber than 'Ho-Ho's.'"

"Ha-ha."

"Are you picking on me?" Before I could answer she said: "Never mind. Let's be serious. How are we going to go about this?"

"Walk in there and find the sister and get her to tell us where Enrique is."

"It's no wonder you don't have a girlfriend."

"Pardon me?"

"Does the word 'subtlety' mean anything to you?"

"Not very much." That produced a smile.

"I want to do this one. Just me. You got the last one."

Arguing would be useless. "Okay, but I wait outside in the car."

"Deal."

We dropped by 'The Road Home' after class. East Hollywood. Aracely walked in; I stayed on the sidewalk, cell phone in my pocket, gun in my car. Two cigarettes later she emerged, happy.

"It was a breeze. Except I had to tell her who I was."

"What did she say?"

"Enough. She's still upset about losing them, both, and she thinks Carl did it." We walked to my car.

"Why?"

"That she didn't say. I asked her if I could speak with Enrique, would she mind, you know."

"Subtle." I opened the door to let her in. I believe she used the F-word under her breath, or some form of it. I went around to the driver's side and got in, waiting.

"His phone number," she said, patting her purse. We headed toward the Valley.

Enrique didn't answer; Aracely left him a message. Could she speak with him about Yung? Would he meet her somewhere?

He called her before we'd reached my apartment. At first it sounded like he wasn't willing to meet, but then she charmed him, and he agreed. Denny's, on Reseda. In thirty minutes.

"He must live nearby."

She nodded. "What am I asking him? I forgot."

"About the trip to San Francisco--was he aware of it, for starters. Did he go with them, what did they do there..."

"Yeah. Should I mention 'Ha-Ha's'?"

"Ho-Ho's." When I gave her a look, she smiled innocently. "Why not?"

We parked around the corner in case Enrique was watching the lot. I gave her a kiss.

"Be careful. I'll be right outside."

"You could come in."

"He's only expecting you."

"I mean, sit nearby."

"Two things wrong with that: if he knows who I am, and sees me, it'll tip him off, and I'd like to be at the door in case he pulls something or runs out, or...if you call me."

"That's three things."

When she began walking toward the coffee shop I suddenly thought: how will she know who he is? I followed a moment later, with my gun in my pocket, starting to regret the whole idea. She went inside; I stopped near the door, lit a cigarette, and strolled away.

Enrique, or someone I thought was Enrique, entered a few minutes later. Through the window I saw him look around and walk to her table, stand for a second, and sit. They shook hands. A waitress took what I assumed were drink orders. Enrique was glancing to his side and behind him, but I couldn't move away, even if he saw me. I couldn't let her out of my sight.

They talked, they drank coffee, I smoked.

He was shaking his head repeatedly, and shrugging. At one point he laughed. Aracely appeared calm, smiling, nonchalant. Then he leaned back, pointed his finger at her, stood up, pulled a bill from his pocket, tossed it on the table, turned, and left. She sat demurely, so I edged forward to watch him exit the coffee shop, jump in a red Mustang, and drive off. I couldn't read the license plate; the police could dig it up, anyway.

Inside I joined her, feeling anxious but good. "How'd it go?"

"Whew," she exhaled, "that was exciting!"

"You looked so calm."

"Well, I wasn't."

The waitress came up. Before she spoke I said: "Coffee, please."

"More for you?" she asked Aracely.

"Can I switch to decaf?"

"Decaf? Of course." She took her cup away, ignoring Enrique's half-filled one.

"He denied everything. Wait--is it smart for us to stay here?" She glanced to the front.

"No, but if we go we can be spotted, also."

"We could leave separately."

"I don't believe it's worth bothering."

A busboy brought her decaf and my regular.

"Hungry?"

She gave me a puzzled look. "I have no appetite. None."

"Hey, you did good."

"Thanks. But he denied knowing anything about the trip, about the bar, about the kinky stuff."

"You asked him?"

"I did."

"Brave."

She drank some decaf.

"Or dumb," I said, smiling.

"Fu--"

"Don't."

"Okay."

I drank my coffee. "Come on, give, give."

"Well...I got the impression he was telling the truth. But I also think he knows more than he let on. He got mad when I pushed him about that sex ring business."

"Sex ring?"

"Well, what do you want to call it?"

"Okay."

"He got so mad he left."

"I saw that."

"Where were you, anyway?"

"Next to that tree." I pointed through the window behind us.

"Cool. I say he was upset because he knew all about it, and he didn't want Yung involved in it."

"Puts him up there with Carl."

"Yes. Well, not exactly, but up there."

"Now what?"

She drank more decaf. "Your turn."

"There's a chance he wasn't lying."

"I just said that, I just said I didn't think he--"

"Right. Okay...so it wasn't him, in San Francisco, in the bar."

"Who was it?"

My turn to take a sip. "Not Miko."

"Duh." I reached under the table and squeezed her knee. "Stop it!" I did, saying:

"It was someone we don't know about, obviously. A client, or...a friend of hers, or somebody she picked up, or picked her up."

"Keep going." I reached under the table. "Not that, mister. Keep talking."

"Someone like...an old boyfriend of Genie's."

10

In the morning I took a shower, made a cup of instant coffee, wondered when I would resume my exercise routine, and called Aracely at work.

"Detective Figari would like to see us in his office as soon as we can manage it," she informed me.

"Why?"

"Your guess is as good as mine."

She said she could get off work early, so I tried to study, briefing a case for Intro using the basic formula, dressed and drove to the OK Skin Care building. Aracely zoomed out, looking tired and spirited at the same time. Inner spirit, outer fatigue.

I attempted to kiss her but she brushed it off. "Ed, take it easy." She settled into the front seat, straightened her jacket, put her knees together, looked forward. So I asked:

"Afraid we'll be seen?"

"Yes!" I drove downtown. After a while I asked:

"How was work?"

"Sucky."

"The boss? I thought he was leaving you alone."

"He is, don't worry. And he hired a new masseuse. But--listen to this." I started to light a cigarette, but her look forestalled me. "Miko took off. Vanished without a word."

"Huh?"

"So Carl told me."

"That's weird. Maybe Carl--oh, no."

"Killed him, too? That's what I thought at first, except he's awfully upset about it. Not like pretending to be."

We sat, thinking. Aracely beat me to it: "He could have split after the detective questioned him. Probably what happened."

"<u>Did</u> he question him?

"He was going to. You know that!" She was uptight. I let it go. We reached the Sheriff's Department, parked in the underground structure, passed through the metal detector (fortunately I had put my gun in the trunk), and proceeded anxiously to Figari's division--homicide.

Several desks in a very large office. Not much activity. One plainclothes officer at his desk, on the phone. One young couple leaving, distraught looks on their faces. I realized we must have looked exactly the same, going in.

Figari stood when he saw us. He had a gun under his windbreaker, not very well hidden, and a badge on his belt, under his big belly. But he looked powerful.

"Hello, you two. Sit down." We all shook hands, we all sat down, he behind his cluttered desk. I had met him before, but now Figari looked oddly different. Too much pressure?

He waved a folder at us. "Found an old complaint against Carl Donahue. Assault and Battery. <u>Sexual</u> battery. Five years ago."

"Wow," Aracely offered. "What happened?"

"Can't tell you. Sorry. But for the fact that it's in keeping with the special equipment you heard he uses. You know."

She nodded. "And?"

He dropped the folder on his desk for emphasis.

"Charges dropped?" My contribution. He looked at me, nodded a little, and then frowned. "Can't say." He peeked over his shoulder at a door marked 'Lieutenant Dezes.'
"I'm in trouble as it is due to you guys. The lieutenant

is very understanding, I'm lucky. But he draws the line here."

"Sure," I said. "We get it." Figari started to say something else but I continued: "Let's give _you_ a piece of information. We saw Enrique." When he puckered his brow I said: "Yung's boyfriend. We--well, _she_--" I glanced at Aracely "--talked with him. Last night."

She said: "You know, that bartender said he'd been in there with Genie, drunk, and he'd thrown him out? But Enrique claimed it wasn't him, that he didn't go up there."

Figari shifted his gaze to me. "Didn't the bartender identify him?"

"Not really. Just her. _I_ called him Enrique, I--wait a second. I said was he, you know, Spanish-looking. He said yes. But it might be another man."

"Uh-huh. No photo of Enrique?"

"Yung worked at 'The Road Home.' Maybe Genie's sister has one."

"Uh-huh."

Aracely said: "I spoke with _her_, too."

Figari chuckled. "Big surprise." His phone rang. He gestured to an officer at a desk nearby who punched a button and answered it.

"What's the age of the man in the bar? The Spanish-looking man with Genie?"

"I forgot to ask about that. It seemed like--"

"Don't sweat it." Figari wrote on a notepad. I was embarrassed. Aracely didn't say a word. In a moment he looked up at us. "I have to talk to Enrique again, and get his photo to this--Hal. See if he'll identify him."

I asked: "Do you know who Genie's old boyfriend is? Maybe he's Latino."

"I know about him." Figari pushed some papers around, then gave up looking. "I know him."

"Detective," Aracely began, "Carl said his bodyguard Miko has disappeared. He told me this morning."

The detective contemplated this, but made no comment. I was getting uneasy. A policewoman entered and crossed to her desk. She wore a short skirt and a holstered gun over a frilly top. Figari watched her sit, a twinkle in his eye, and looked back at us.

"I advise you not to discuss this with Donahue. As a matter of fact, I advise you to leave it all alone. Call me if you have any ideas, but don't act on your own." He sighed when we gave no response. "I'll check out Miko.

I'll check out the sister. Okay? I'll check with the bartender."

Aracely said: "Great. Thanks. You know we appreciate everything you're doing." She meant it.

Outside, the afternoon was edging toward evening. We decided to eat and go to class. Tacos from a lunch wagon set up near City Hall. There was sadness in her eyes. Were we getting anywhere with this, aside from placing Detective Figari in an uncomfortable position?

I put an arm around her as we walked to my car. "Do you have all your stuff for class? You'll never make it to Glendale and back in time."

"Enough stuff."

We drove to the salon, she got her car, and we each drove to the school, with fifteen minutes to spare. I was growing sad myself. If Carl did it, how can we prove it?

She went to her Property class, I to my Intro. The three hours dragged, but fortunately my professor let us go early. I waited for her outside the building. She showed up with another student.

"This is Maribel. This is Eddie."

I said: "Oh, Hi!" Maribel was short and even younger than Aracely. Now I was 'Eddie.'

"You guys are mixed up in a murder case?"

I forced a laugh, attempting to make light of it. "Sort of. We're helping the police."

"Must be exciting. Aracely said you met with the police today."

"Yeah, and he warned us to keep out of it."

Aracely adjusted her bag on her shoulder. "Eddie doesn't want to leave it alone. Do you, Eddie?"

"Yes and no."

"Who did it? She won't tell me anything!"

"There's one strong suspect. Her boss at work."

Maribel's eyes showed fear. "Watch out!"

"He may not be the one," I quickly added.

"Are you guys kidding about this?"

"No," Aracely said. "It's no joke. Somebody stabbed two women to death, and one of them worked for me--with me. I don't know why--we don't know why, except my boss was selling her, and--"

"Selling her? Her body, you mean?"

"Uh-huh. She'd let herself get tied up, handcuffed, something like that, and blindfolded, I guess, and men would have sex with her."

Maribel's mouth dropped open.

"My boss was making her do it."

"For money?"

"Guess so."

"Why don't they arrest him?"

I said: "Not enough to go on. We can't prove it. Her boss has to make an admission, or confess, or...make a mistake."

"This is incredible," Maribel said.

"I know, but Eddie and I don't want to give up. Do we?"

"No."

"Want to help?" Aracely asked her. I shook my head but Maribel said:

"Yes! I'd like to. Only..."

"Only don't ask her that, it's dangerous," I imposed. "We're crazy to be mixed up in it. Don't ask someone else, you--"

"He's right. Never mind, Maribel. It's too dangerous. We are crazy. Anything can happen."

"We don't even know what to do next," I said. "Do we?"

Aracely laughed. "Not actually."

"Well, let me know. Call me tomorrow. I'll get here early. I want to know everything."

Aracely looked at me. I nodded, reluctantly. "We certainly could use some new ideas."

That's how we left it. Figures a law student couldn't resist getting involved. At Aracely's Range Rover we kissed, briefly. Her body felt warm.

"I need a good night's sleep," she said.

"That's subtle."

"Are you angry?"

"I'm kidding. I can't keep up with you anyway." She hugged me.

11

That night I had two beers, watched the news, turned off the TV and tried to think over the Intro lecture. I'd turned in my brief. The professor's style was to discuss our assignment, through class participation, and then explain the law that fit the case. I hadn't raised my hand except once when no one wanted to take a position opposite Victor's. I didn't get very far, though.

This murder investigation was wearing me down. Aracely had looked so unhappy after our discussion with Figari that I began to lose enthusiasm. We needed a new avenue to explore. But what? The detective was planning on covering all the points we'd advanced. What else was there to do?

I went to bed drowning in hopelessness, with visions of Genie, my encounter with her, the long night of finding the bodies, sitting in the police station, the ensuing trips to Ventura and San Francisco, to the bar on Beverly, the wait outside the coffee shop watching Enrique. So what if he got mad about the 'sex ring' accusation? Who wouldn't?

I got up and took two homeopathic relaxation tablets-- 'Calms.' They worked.

In the morning it came to me: the ex-boyfriend. Had to find him. Unless Hal identifies a photo of Enrique. In that event maybe they were <u>all</u> guilty: Donahue, Miko, Enrique.

No forced entry. No 'breaking-and-entering.' Why didn't the neighbors hear screaming? Of course they <u>must</u> have, but were afraid to report it later because they hadn't done a thing to help.

I called Figari.

"Say, the more I think about it, the more I wonder who Genie's boyfriend was. What do you have on him?"

"I have a name. I talked to him at his workplace, uh, two weeks ago. Why?"

"Why? Maybe he was with her at Ho-Ho's, that's why. Maybe he blew a gasket when he heard about the sex parties, and stabbed them. I think it's plausible."

"That doesn't explain Miko running off."

"No. He ran because of, uh, well, his complicity in the bondage scene. That's illegal, isn't it?"

"If money changed hands."

"There you go," I said.

"Stay out of it. I'll handle it."

I shifted gears fast. "What about that hot policewoman in the office?"

"What about her?"

"I mean, is she on this case?"

"Not directly, no. We happen to have other homicides. It's a big city. If--"

"I know, Detective. We're very grateful for the attention you've been giving this, it's--"

"Stay out of it. I'm not trying to be tough on you two, really. Call me anytime you think of something."

"Is the lieutenant listening to you right now?"

"Correct."

"Okay. I'll talk to you later."

"Whatever happens is what happens." Why I was thinking that when I first saw Aracely, I don't know. She'd caught my eye when we all stood up, and altered my thought process. Not to mention my life.

Maribel was in the student lounge with her when I arrived at school. I joined them. They were sitting on the long couch, their bags on the equally long table. I said Hello and got a 50¢ cup of coffee from a vending machine and sat beside Aracely.

"Ready for Torts?" She only smirked in response to my question.

"Guess what?" Maribel asked me.

"What?"

"You tell him."

Aracely took a deep breath. "Today I pulled out Genie's work application. Her most recent employer was Regency Spa in Sherman Oaks. I called them on a pretext, that I felt they should know what had happened to her."

"Very good. And?"

"The receptionist hadn't known. She became upset, because she remembered Genie. She called her 'Lee,' of course. That's the name on the application. But--"

"You're positive Genie is Lee?"

"Yes, positive."

"Go on."

She looked at Maribel, who was so excited I wanted to laugh. Maribel said: "The receptionist asked if 'Bo' knew about what happened."

"I said: 'He may not. Perhaps you might pass it on to him, considering <u>their past relationship</u>.' She told me she would."

"Is Bo who I think he is?"

Aracely smiled a big one. "Has to be! Why else would the woman mention him?"

Maribel interjected: "Absolutely."

"Bo might just be the boss. He'd need to be informed, she may--"

"Uh-uh! I brought that up, and the receptionist said she'd have to tell <u>her</u>, too. The 'manager.' A woman."

"This Bo is a masseur," Maribel said. "I called to make an appointment. I asked for a man." There was no way I couldn't laugh at that. But I was alarmed, nevertheless:

"You can't go in there."

"And why not?"

"Come on, Maribel. You going to ask if he killed them?"

"Do I look stupid?"

"No," I said quickly. "I mean, what do you hope to find out without talking too much? You'd have to say <u>something</u> about the murders."

Two students had come in and gone to the vending machines. Aracely spoke in a low voice:

"She won't say anything. Just size him up."

"What good will that do? It's risky."

Aracely smiled at the two other students. I had to nod Hello to them. They sat down at a table twenty feet away, talking and eating. Maribel whispered:

"I suppose you want to take the appointment?" Aracely laughed at that. She had me there.

"No way." They both laughed at me. "Hey, I wouldn't be comfortable, that's all."

"Well, I can't take the appointment," Aracely whispered. "He may know who I am."

"Don't reveal anything." Maribel and I were sitting in my car near the Regency Spa. She began to laugh after I said it.

"Anything?" Not until she left to walk up the street did I understand the way she took it. My sense of humor was suffering under the strain. I lit a cigarette, feeling like Humphrey Bogart, watching her enter and disappear, wondering if she'd be alright.

She had a cell phone, but couldn't very well hide it under the towel. What if he pulled it off, as Genie had done during my massage?

Ten minutes, twenty minutes. I got out and walked up and down. I checked my phone to make sure it was on, although I knew it was. I told myself this wasn't the killer, anyway. Why did I suspect him at all? Hal will identify a photo of Enrique, and that would be the end of it.

Forty minutes, fifty minutes. I decided to go in if she didn't emerge exactly on time. The gun was still in the trunk. If I got it now a pedestrian or passing motorist could see, and maybe call 911. I went to the door, had another cigarette, which tasted terrible, and entered.

But Maribel was there, paying the cashier with a credit card, looking happy.

She turned and walked past me without any acknowledgment. Smart, except the cashier stared at me steadily until I walked out, feeling stupid.

Maribel had turned the other direction, so I got to my car and followed, made the corner and picked her up.

"How exciting!" she gushed. "It was Bo, of course, which they'd already said yesterday, but I couldn't be positive, you know, until I got in there. And he was normal, you know, like he had no idea why I came in, except to get a massage."

"How was it?"

She didn't miss a beat. "Good! I mean, I had to tell him not that much pressure. They always think you want a 'deep-tissue' one. Cute guy, too, lots of muscles."

"Okay, okay. Did you mention Genie?"

"What? Of course I didn't! But I thought up a good subject for conversation. Remember that movie 'Psycho'?"

Later, before class, Maribel explained it again to Aracely, in the lounge, going over every detail. By that time I had grown to accept it. If he was suspicious, so be it.

"I told him I'd watched it on cable not too long ago, that I was only taking baths, now, that it had frightened me, and--"

Aracely interrupted: "What did he say?"

"It had scared him, too. Particularly when the man was stabbed going up the staircase. But I brought him around to the dead woman again, how clever it was to sink her body in the pond, how most people just leave a body where they'd stabbed it, but that--"

"What was his reaction?"

"Nothing. Like it was nothing important."

I put my head in my hands.

At eight, during the break, I searched for Maribel. She wasn't taking Torts, but I found her outside a classroom downstairs, eager as ever.

"Hi, Eddie!"

"Hi. Uh, I forgot to ask you: is he Latin-looking? You know, Hispanic?"

"Huh? Oh...yes, as a matter of fact. Why?"

It was out of my way, but I dropped in for a beer at 'The Road Home.' Not surprisingly, a photo of Genie was on the wall, alongside a photo of Yung. Or so the barmaid informed me. Genie's sister was off that night. I stared at the faces on the wall, drank half the beer, and left.

I knew my life was united with those two girls, forever, no matter how it unfolded. In the beginning, Aracely was the motivation. Now it was them, this wickedness done to them. My heart was with two people who had distantly crossed my path, one I'd not even met. Seeing the photo of Jung, her artless face, her gentle expression, caused a major shift inside my being. Genie and Yung, whoever they really were, had had a future. Now they had none. Were they in heaven? I hoped so, but didn't know. If so, more power to them. But they'd lost their chance, here, they'd had it stolen away, against their wills. Whoever had done it had no right to pursue his own future unchallenged, anymore. He had to be caught.

There was a good movie, a Chinese movie, called "The Road Home." The story of a woman who struggled to attain a promising future. Maybe the bar was named after that movie, maybe not. Maybe those two dead girls would have attained a beautiful future, maybe not. As I parked behind my apartment I recalled Genie's unpretentious face, too, heard her say: "Oh, no, we don't do that here," or whatever it was she'd told me; I couldn't remember exactly. But she'd been determined to live, as Yung must have been. It was only right to find out what happened, to keep it from happening again.

I wanted to talk to Aracely, but it was late. Could have sent an e-mail, if I had the setup. One more new-

fangled invention I resisted. What was I hanging on to?
Get with it, Ed. Join the 21st Century.

I didn't call her. I heated up the meatloaf my part-time housekeeper had put in the fridge. Genie and Yung, Genie and Yung. I sat and ate, thinking of them, thinking of a way to solve the case. No good ideas came to me, so I went to bed, feeling lonely.

12

Not knowing what to do next, I got a newspaper and broached the subject with Lefty. As I'd expected, the former journalist was aware of the murders.

"Cops can't solve it, eh?"

"No."

"Why do you care?"

"One girl I knew. The other was okay, too. It's a bad deal. I feel sad for them."

"Edward, girls are everywhere."

"It's not that. It was a brutal crime, it can't be tolerated."

"Listen to you. I hope this wasn't the one you told me about. The heartbreaker."

"No." A customer making a purchase diverted his attention. After the transaction Lefty gazed into the street.

"One time an Asian woman was kidnapped. I heard, only heard, mind you, it was the Mob."

"Skip it. Too dangerous."

"There's more, Edward. A wannabe was holding her. The Mob hadn't liked it, don't ask me why."

"Why?"

"I said--ha-ha, such a kidder. Anyway, they freed her, the wannabe escaped with a beating. Still uses a cane. Does drugs now and then."

"Selling?"

"That's what I hear." Another customer, a raggedy near-street-woman, bought a magazine.

"Are you implying I ought to speak with this dude with the cane?"

"It's an angle. Might be a connection."

"You haven't told me all you know."

"I haven't, that's a fact."

The wannabe wasn't a wannabe now. He'd learned his lesson. Lefty pointed me to him. Underside of L.A., what used to be 'Skid Row,' but was now discount furnitureville. Broken-down area between high-rises and factories, closer to the factories. 'Frome,' so his name was, assisted the owner of a used clothing store. I needed a new jacket, anyway.

Well, it wasn't 'new,' but it was cheap, and I struck up a conversation with the clerk, a man with a cane. I told him I sold items at the swap meet at the fairgrounds.

"You could get rid of this stuff there."

"Talk to the owner."

"No, not me sell it, you could sell it. Lots of people every weekend. Saturday's the busiest."

"You have a booth?"

"Vending booth. Steady sales."

"Want a commission?"

"I don't want a fucking thing." Picked it up from Aracely.

Frome slowly sat in a chair, his bad leg stretched out. No customers.

"What do you want, then?" Hard case.

"As a matter of fact, the more clothing vendors, the more people may want my stuff. We have a few T-shirts and sweatshirts. Mostly posters, car models, photos. But a few clothing articles." Where was I going with this?

"The owner could be interested. I'll let him know. What's your name?"

"Ed."

"Frome." We shook. He stood up, took his cane, and walked with me to the front. It was wide open, tables exposed to the sidewalk. There was a hot dog stand across the street.

"Want one?" I asked, pointing to it. "I'm going to get one."

"Shit, yeah."

He sat in his chair to eat it. Two black teenagers, probably brother and sister, the way they talked, selected an armful of old shirts and pants. When they were ready Frome rang it up, took their money, thanked them.

I had an idea, so I tried it:

"Did I see you at the OK Skin Care place? A month ago? No, longer."

"OK Skin Care?"

"Massage parlor. On Serrano."

Bingo. "Shit, yeah. I been in a bunch of times." He gave me a suspicious look and a half-smile.

"Yeah," I laughed. "I saw you. Good place except I had to get two massages before I got a handjob."

"They're like that." The suspicion left, the smile broadened. "Gotta get to know you."

"I was just in last week. There's a new masseuse. Cute, too. Angie, I think."

"Don't know her. I stopped going since...do you know about what happened? To Genie?"

Hearing the name made my adrenaline go. I wouldn't be able to lie about it convincingly, so I said: "Oh yeah. I heard. It was in the paper. Too bad." He didn't say anything, and another customer needed attention. Questions about the jackets. Mine was in a bag on the counter. I thought: now's the time, Edward. Go for it.

The woman didn't buy a jacket, and left. Frome adjusted a pile of shirts, appeared to be thinking something over because he took too long.

I moved to the front to have a cigarette, formulating my next comment. Frome limped over to me, his cane tapping the concrete floor. He said it for me:

"The other deal, that's expensive, huh?"

I looked at him as knowingly as I could. "Never went for it, but wanted to. How much they get, anyway?"

"Never did it? Come on, Ed. Don't bullshit an old bullshitter."

"I'm not," I laughed as pleasantly as I could manage. "The one I had was offering after a couple more times, that's all. Really." He appeared to accept it. "I should have asked how much. What is it, three hundred, or what?"

"You'll have to ask them." Smart punk.

"I'm going to. I'll ask Angie. Can't afford it now, whatever the fuck it is. Come on, man, how much do they want? Like, say, for a half-hour?"

He shook his head, but asked: "You want the whole nine yards?"

"Why not? I saw pictures of it, but I never tried it."

"I can get you someone, cheaper than that place. And you won't have to go out of town."

"Now you're talking!" The words just popped out, and I felt embarrassed, and nervous.

"Two hundred for half an hour. The whole nine yards."

"We talking about the same thing?" I put my hands behind my back, like I was handcuffed, and then gestured to my legs as though tying a rope around. He nodded.

"Nice girl?"

"You won't be disappointed."

Ten minutes and one more customer later, it was all arranged. A hotel room downtown. <u>Way</u> downtown, the next day. Fifty dollars in advance. Her name was Kari, half-Hawaiian, half-black. I was to call him first, show up at noon.

If I went through with it I could pry more information out of him, get closer to the truth. It smelled right. He was mixed up in it, no doubt. Maybe all the way.

Aracely hated the idea, of course. Not because it was perverse, as I expected, but because of the danger. Also it may have hurt her feelings.

"There's no danger. <u>That</u> comes when I press him for more information."

"This is going too far. I don't like it."

"What are you talking about?"

"String him along, but don't have sex with her."

"If it bothers you, I'll cancel the appointment."

"That what you're calling it? An appointment?"

"Aracely, how come you--" I stopped, realizing her feelings <u>were</u> hurt. "This is only a way to discover more. Sex isn't the issue."

"I'm sorry, Ed. I'm a woman. I can't--"

"Yes you are, so I'll cancel. Screw it."

Silence. I wanted to ask why she cared so much. We weren't boyfriend and girlfriend. I wanted to ask if Roy apologized, wouldn't she go back to him? But I waited.

"Okay," she finally said. "Don't do it."

"Okay."

"Fine."

"It's nothing to me."

"Me either."

"I'll tell him to forget it."

"You wouldn't want _me_ to, if it was the other way around. Would you?"

Time to lie? Lies had ended my marriage. "Honestly, I'd let you, but for the risk."

"You said there wasn't any risk!"

"I meant not for me. You'd be too vulnerable."

"You wouldn't care otherwise?"

Another temptation to lie, to make her feel good.

"Certainly I'd care." That was the truth. "Only I'm twice your age. I have no right to you. We aren't boyfriend and girlfriend. We--"

"So what? You wouldn't care?"

"I'd live with it."

"Oh!" She hung up on me.

That following the Frome lead had potential seemed more than obvious, so I held off canceling. Dealing with

Aracely also seemed necessary. I didn't want to lose her friendship. But how to patch it up?

She ignored me in class, no matter how much I looked at her. Women. Like a different species entirely.

I smoked alone, near my car, during the break. Our relationship was more important to me than our stumbling investigation, no matter how compelling it was. After class, gathering up my books, I said:

"Tomorrow I'll call and tell him no."

She refused to speak, but did sigh. It was an opening.

"Frome's not going to confide in me anyway," I added.

She loaded her bag and walked away, but then paused at the door, smiling at other students as they exited. When I approached, Aracely gave me that vaguely amused look of hers.

"No, do it. He'll trust you after that."

"Are you sure?"

"We can't quit now."

"Aracely...are you sure it's okay?"

"Just go ahead, will you?"

Now the only question was, could I go through with it?
Suppose I couldn't perform? Suppose I got arrested and the
state bar hears? That would mean the end of my law career.

13

In the morning I woke up early and talked myself around my fears. This Kari was the way to access Frome. Otherwise he wouldn't tell me anything. For all he knew I was an undercover policeman, after him and his operation. Or for the murders. If I go through with this he'll trust me; that's what I told myself on the way over.

She wasn't so pretty, but very exotic. Torn blue jeans, shirt open to the waist. Yikes.

My guess was Frome was nearby, perhaps in another room. With a gun and a knife and a blackjack.

She asked me for the $150 right away. She laid out a skimpy array of paraphernalia, put music on, sat on the bed and said:

"Whatever you want."

I did the best I could. Afterward, in my car, glad to be away from that fleabag hotel, glad to be alive, I decided when I was an attorney I'd represent hookers. Ought to be legal, anyway, with legitimate businessmen running it. Or businesswomen. Paying taxes. Licenses. Medical examinations and permits.

Aracely called. I had to answer.

"Are you alright?"

"I'm fine. No problems."

"Did you like her?"

Obviously Lefty knew the guy had a connection to OK Skin Care, and the girls. But there was no reasonable way I could question Lefty, now. Anything I said might end up getting to Frome, accidentally or otherwise.

That night, after class, drinking beer, I felt sympathy for Figari. Not being able to trust anyone fully, always on guard, forever staying one step ahead of potential suspects. What a job. If you reveal too much to one person, another can hear about it, and the investigation is compromised. I decided to keep Aracely away from Frome. Didn't want her to get hurt.

But how to proceed? If I call him too soon and ask about Genie, he'll catch on. In the morning I resolved to wait as long as I could stand it.

Where was Geraldo Rivera when you needed him? The press had dropped the case as fast as it had grabbed it up. Nothing on TV, nothing in the paper.

In Intro I learned you have to intend to commit a felony, or 'any theft crime,' statutorily, for breaking-and-entering to be a burglary. That was a relief. All we'd done was examine that 'sex lounge'...no felonious 'intent.' I dared to ask the professor:

"What's the crime if there's no intent to commit a felony, or to steal anything?"

"If intent is formed <u>after</u> entering, and something is taken, it's 'larceny.'"

"Well, what if nothing is taken?"

"Who can answer that?" Our professor looked around the classroom, and called on Victor.

"The breaking-and-entering is still unlawful."

"Under which condition would it be unlawful?"

"If it's trespassing...without consent."

There was a hint of a smile on the professor's lips. "Oh, I can't wait to grade your exam."

"<u>Trespassory</u>," Victor amended quickly. A few of the students laughed.

"In this case it also happens to be 'trespassing,' you're right. But by accident." He smiled and turned to the class:

"In this hypothetical, suppose our perpetrator opened a drawer, or a closet, in search of something, but didn't find it?" He looked at the 40ish woman in the back.

"That's...there's intent, so it's burglary."

"Was there intent?" he asked. I was growing more and more uncomfortable: we had opened the cabinet 'in search of something.'

"Yes. He opened a drawer, looking to steal something," she responded.

"Maybe not," the professor corrected. "Maybe he didn't open the drawer to steal anything. Then what?"

The black woman in the front row had her hand up, but the professor nodded at me:

"It's your hypothetical."

"Like Victor said, they--he--still committed a crime. Just not burglary."

"And who determines whether or not there was intent? The defendant?" He called on the black woman, who always knew the right answer.

"No, that's up to the jury to determine."

It rained hard that night. Storms often hit Los Angeles like that, coming in from the North Pacific Ocean.

Robert had worried about an occasional drop over the weekend; he should be pleased the rain held off until now. I couldn't have cared less. Local weather reports predicted the storm would be gone by Saturday, so people would show up at the fairgrounds. Perhaps Frome would show up, threatening me.

No, no. He didn't have a clue what I was up to. I hadn't said anything to Kari about it, although I'd dearly wanted to ask if she'd known Genie.

I spoke with Aracely during the day, Tuesday. We had to devise a plan regarding Frome. But I'd do the legwork. She pressured me to admit the session in the hotel room was 'exciting.'

"Don't expect me to do that with you."

"I hope you're joking. I wouldn't ask you to--"

"I'm not joking. Don't get any ideas."

"How about me wearing the handcuffs?"

"Hmmm...it's a thought," she said.

"While you're thinking, tell me this: is it better to phone or go to that garment store in person?"

"Go...in person. Yeah. Face to face."

"Explaining I need time to earn enough money for the next session, that I liked it, that--"

"Don't overdo it."

"Just explaining, making it up."

"I hope so."

"Touchy, touchy."

"Shut up." I did. "If you talk about the girls, just pretend you aren't bothered, that you don't care they died."

"Not bothered?"

"A little, okay. But if he's the one who did it, you want to disarm him."

"True."

"And say you enjoy getting rough, that Kari wasn't fighting enough."

"She didn't fight at all."

"Shut up."

I walked into the shop Wednesday. Frome was there. And more customers than I expected, considering the rain. Regrettably the owner was out, again. I wanted to meet him, to carry on the charade of his having a booth next to mine.

During a free moment Frome asked, of course, if Kari had been 'satisfactory.' I told him yes, that I wanted a repeat, after I'd put together more money.

"You've got my number. It's best not to come around here."

"Right. Got you." Supposing he'd rather I leave, I worked fast: "Wish Genie was around. She was alright."

"Prefer an Asian?"

"No. Yes. I don't care. You have any?"

"Not now. Somebody bumped them off."

"No offense, but weren't they Donahue's?"

"Yeah, but they worked for me, on the side."

"Good deal. Hey, they come and go. If you find another one, I'm interested."

"One like Genie?" It vaguely troubled me how he said it, but I pushed ahead:

"Doesn't matter. What did she do, piss off a client?"

"She pissed off somebody."

"Yeah. Should have been more careful."

He actually laughed. "The other one too."

It was all I could stand. "Well, gotta go. Traffic's bad in the rain." Not wanting to shake his hand, I backed away, waving. But, remembering Aracely's advice, I stepped forward, to shake. "Thanks again."

Two days later he left a message on my cell phone, in the middle of the night: "Call me. I got what you requested." What a low-life.

I told him I would have to see her first, so we set up a rendezvous: me, the girl, and him. I had come up with a plan, of sorts.

We met at Norm's in Hollywood, Saturday night. Frome even wore a sports coat. Mr. Business. The Asian woman appeared nervous, so I told her she wouldn't have to do anything she felt uncomfortable doing.

"We'll have fun. Don't worry." Now I was a low-life.

"It's gonna cost a little more, Ed. She's new at it."

"So?"

"She wants a bigger cut. Take it or leave it."

"How much?"

"Three hundred."

"Okay. But I don't have it yet."

"Sure, I know." My plan was working.

We ate steak. I paid. The woman, Kim, only finished half of hers. I felt sorry for her, and outside, said: "If you don't want to, just tell me. I understand."

"I want to."

"She'll do it," Frome insisted. I gave her a kiss on the cheek in the parking lot. Kim had come in her own car, a dented Honda. We waved as she drove away, and walked to Frome's undented SUV. I lit a smoke and growled:

"This isn't going to work, man. I need one I can get rough with."

"She's gonna be fine. How rough?"

"You know."

"Hell I do. How rough?"

"What do you care? She'll survive."

"Are you crazy? I'm calling it off."

"Easy, pard. After what you did to those two girls, this is nothing much."

"What I--?" He stepped away from me, nearly dropping his cane. "That's crazy. I didn't do that. I'm..."

"What?"

"Ask Detective Figari about it."

"Huh?"

"Ask Detective Figari," he repeated, and laughed. "You dumb shit." He used his remote to unlock his door and climbed in awkwardly. "Only don't say a word about our little arrangement."

Aracely wasn't pleased. Not only did she not want me to come over, she said I was 'reckless.'

"Granted."

"You were supposed to trap him into an admission, not make him blow up!"

"Well, it's a fine line. You try it."

She was quiet, and in a moment said:

"I wonder what Figari has to do with it. Can you reach him now?"

"I'd rather wait until tomorrow. They'll patch me through if I push it hard enough."

"Push. But remember, don't you dare mention the 'arrangement.'"

"What's that, me and Kari?"

"Duh."

"Okay. Are you sure you trust me to handle it?"

At last, a small giggle. "Yes. I'm sorry I yelled at you."

"Don't worry about it. Can I come over now?"

"You have to work in the morning."

"That's a 'no'?"

"That's a 'maybe you can come over another night.'"

"Tomorrow night?" She didn't answer.

They put me through to the detective.

"Must be great having weekends off. How'd you swing that?"

"Years on the force. Seniority. What's up?"

"Do you know a character named Frome?"

Rather than play games with me, he said:

"I know him. Small-time drug dealer. Dick Frome."

"Yeah, bad leg?"

"Uh-huh. Why?"

"He knew Genie and Yung."

"Yes?"

"Could he have killed them?"

"Why?" Now he was playing games.

"Just asking." I could do it, too.

"Ed. Spit it out."

"I talked to him. I hinted he may have killed them. He blew up and told me to ask you."

"Sure. He's an informant."

"Wow. But...how's it fit together? I mean, he thought it was funny, my speaking to you."

"Frome's a creep who tells us where the drugs are--what's this about? Not the drug supply."

"No. Nothing to do with that, far as I know. Unless the girls were buying them. It's what he said: 'Ask Figari.'"

A split-second pause, a sigh, a lowered voice. "You spread this around, he'll be in jeopardy."

"Don't worry."

"He's in contact with dealers. You say a word, he's gone."

"I understand."

"There was a raid the night of the murders. Remember Officer Pechenco? The woman in our office?"

"Sure."

"She and I assisted in the raid. Frome was with us the whole night. Narco and homicide. I won't explain any more. Already told you too much. Suffice it to say he couldn't have done it. Not that he isn't capable of it."

"No wonder he laughed at me. Except...it wasn't: 'speak with a detective name of Figari, Sheriff's homicide division; it was 'ask Figari,' like I knew you."

"He knows it's my case."

"He doesn't know we've discussed it."

"Yes he does. He's an informant. I ran it all down to him. Narcotics was interested in Donahue. Frome worked his way inside, and I knew it. I told him to keep his eyes and ears open regarding those murders. Had to tell him too much, like I'm telling you too much."

"So he knows about Aracely?"

"What do you think?"

Robert noticed my aggravation when I came into the stall, after the phone conversation. He didn't say much, but he watched me. By the end of the day I'd calmed down, and he said politely:

"If you want to talk, I'm willing."

"Thanks, buddy. I'm okay."

"You wouldn't lie to me?"

"Only under the direst of circumstances."

As per her partial invitation, I showed up at Aracely's, with a bag of pot-roast sandwiches from Carrow's and a six-pack of Pacifico. None of the news fazed her. What's to worry? A police informant was engaged in illegal sex traffic, I had taken part in it, a murderer was on the loose, drugs were flying around, Frome had tangled with organized crime, Figari was telling everyone everything, nobody was getting anywhere. Once more I thought: 'whatever happens is what happens.'

She was reluctant to go to bed, and grilled me:

"Did you use a condom?"

"Always."

"I'm serious. With <u>Kari</u>."

"Oh, yeah, absolutely."

"Did you wash yourself after?"

"Yes, definitely."

"Not feeling odd? Any irritation, any--"

"No. Do I have to get a checkup?"

"You <u>should</u>, but I'll take a chance."

14

For the next few days we attended class, studied, forced ourselves to do assignments. Aracely dropped by, after work Wednesday, and we went to a Mexican restaurant. She told me Carl had had an argument with someone in his office.

"Who was it?"

"Bo."

"Did you see him?"

"Plain as day. Had to let him in. He gave me his name. I guess Carl won the argument because Bo stormed out the front like he wanted to tear the place apart. Carl came out, smiling.

"Did he say anything?"

"Uh-huh. Said he didn't want him as a bodyguard."

"Was that a joke, or what?"

"No. They'd had an interview, of sorts. Carl said he didn't believe in hiring ex-convicts."

"No."

"Yes." She ate, for a moment. I drank my beer, then finished a taco.

"That it?"

"Not quite," she answered, smiling. "It seems that Carl knew him from before, that Miko had roughed him up once. He'd worked for him, at one point."

"Bo had worked for Carl? Doing what?"

"Guess."

"I'll guess. The women."

"The women."

"He said that?"

"What he said was close to it: 'My other business.' He knows I know about it. It's no secret over there."

"And Bo wanted Miko's old job?"

"Sounded like that, yes." She ate a little more. Did this all mean anything? Why had they argued?

"Could you hear what they were saying?"

"No, unfortunately. I was afraid to eavesdrop."

"You, afraid? Ha!"

"Sure, Ed, I didn't want to be standing at the door if it opened!"

"I know, I'm kidding."

"Let's call Figari."

"Alright, but it's not that important. They'd never admit what they've been up to. It's a crime."

"Not about that," she said, banging down her fork. "To see if he sent a picture of Enrique to the bartender. If it wasn't him, it was Bo, right?"

"Right. And then what?"

"Do I have to do all the thinking?"

"You're doing pretty good so far." That placated her.

Somehow Figari had arranged to obtain a photo of Enrique, and a local cop obliged by presenting it to Hal. He reportedly refused to say it was the man with Genie, although there was a 'resemblance.' Not conclusive, yet Figari was satisfied. Most witnesses are uncertain when identifying photos, unless it's a person close to them.

"Does Bo look like Enrique?"

"Not much," Aracely told me. She had phoned with the news. "The detective believes it was Enrique. Why would Bo go to the bar, anyway?"

"Why would anybody do anything?" I replied. Before she could answer I said: "In respect to this case, I mean."

"Yeah, it's fucking crazy. By the way, I told him about their argument. It interested him. You were wrong."

"Thanks."

"Don't be sarcastic."

"You sound like my ex."

"What's she like, anyway?"

"Sweet as can be until she gets mad."

"Did you make her mad?"

"Once or twice."

"Not you."

"Hard to believe, I know."

"How old is she?"

"Close to my age. But she takes vitamins, like me."

"Speaking of that, are you coming over tonight? I can--"

"Sure. Sorry, what can you do?"

"Just about everything. But I was going to say, I can cook dinner again. My mother's recipe."

"Cool. We can study, too."

That was Thursday. We were up late studying, eating, planning the next move, both agreeing we ought to keep Maribel out of it. In bed I tried to be twenty-five again.

"Stay," Aracely said in the morning. "I'll call you from work."

My back hurt, my throat was dry, the old knee injury was flaring up. I slept until my phone rang, but it wasn't Aracely. Wrong number.

On the road, after a shower and coffee, my spirits were high. What we needed was a bit of luck, that's all. The pieces were on the table, all except one. With <u>that</u> one, it would come together.

My part-time housekeeper was working in my apartment. Sometimes she came on Saturday, sometimes Sunday, occasional Friday. I left it up to her. One day a week, what did I care? All I had to do was make sure there were enough quarters for the laundry. And leave her a check, of course.

Aracely didn't call, so I did.

"We're swamped!"

"Carl in?"

"No, thank God."

"No time for lunch?"

"Not now. Call me later."

"Okay. Love you."

Yikes.

That afternoon I read a case concerning a college gymnastics coach who sued for 'emotional distress damages.' Her students had accidentally viewed a tape of their latest competition, a tape which happened to contain a sexual encounter the coach had with her husband. Evidently he had filmed both events. She was forced to turn over the tape to her superiors, exacting a promise it wouldn't be viewed, again. It was, and she sued, but lost.

After a nap I woke up with an idea. Videotapes. Had Carl taped those bondage sessions? That could connect him to Genie and Yung, a link to their murders.

Aracely said she'd been through his office carefully, but would do so again. I drove there to help, but she insisted I wait in my car, keeping a lookout for her boss. When the salon closed she examined the office. No tapes, no DVDs. Most likely at his house, if they existed at all.

I bought her dinner at Hamburger Hamlet. She was quite hungry.

"You know, Figari should get a warrant to search the property in Ventura, and Carl's residence here."

"Fat chance," I remarked.

"He might do it."

"I'll ask him."

Of course he said no. Needed 'probable cause.' I was sorely tempted to reveal we had been in that back room, but, after all, he was the police. Instead I reminded him:

"Aracely is sure there's a room in the garage where those sessions are conducted."

"I know. Ask her to find me an eyewitness." You're talking to one, I thought.

"Let's tell him," I said when I called her. "Screw it."

"I don't care to go to jail, or get kicked out of school, for that matter."

"Good point, very good point."

"Roy came by. He apologized." When I didn't comment, she continued: "Tell me not to see him again."

"Would you like to?"

"Just <u>say</u> it."

"Don't see him anymore."

"Ever?"

"Oh, boy. Okay. Don't see him ever again."

"Do you mean it?"

"Why would I say it if I didn't?"

"You're funny. But really, do you?"

"I mean it for now. You may get tired of me. You may want to get married, have kids." It was her turn to be quiet. "Aracely," I said.

"What?"

"I don't want to be married again."

"What about kids?"

"Are you joking?"

"I'm not joking."

"Kids are alright, but shouldn't we get through law school first?" I was happy she laughed.

15

Saturday she called me at work, from the salon: Carl acting 'strangely.' So what else was new?

"Come over for a massage. I want to see you."

"What's the matter?"

"I just don't feel right. I'm worried."

"Want me to come now? I can get away, if you're really feeling weird. You're psychic, remember?"

"Come over."

Robert was fine about it. The sky was gloomy and it wasn't too busy. Looked like rain.

I put my .38 in my jacket pocket. I'd had it with Carl.

On the drive over I kept wondering: what's the last piece of the puzzle? Organized crime? Drugs? Maybe I should ask Maribel.

I had a massage. Aracely behaved coolly, which was proper. I didn't see Carl. The new masseuse was good. She even brushed against my genitals a couple of times. But I was in no mood, praying my jacket and gun didn't fall from its hook on the wall, causing a commotion. In the shower I imagined the masseuse going through my pockets, reporting to Mr. Donahue.

Aracely took my money. The hairdressers were kind of curious; they knew who I was.

"I'm going downstairs for a cup of coffee," I said.

"Join you in ten minutes."

It took fifteen, but she was there.

"I guess everything is fine. He's still in his office." She had coffee, herself, for a change.

"How was he behaving, by the way?"

"I don't know. Curt. Even with customers."

"Maybe he's cracking under the strain."

"How was your massage?"

"Good. But it reminds me of the last time."

"Oh. Yeah." She frowned, glancing at the menu.

"Get a sandwich. You need to eat."

"I'll get it to go."

Aracely was obviously distressed. She got a sandwich, and we stood by the stairs, neither wanting to part company.

"I can wait here. I don't mind."

"Yes, I know. You're wonderful. It'll be okay, now. Just wait at your place. Don't go out."

In my apartment I kept my shoes on, kept my jacket and gun handy. Couldn't concentrate on my Torts notes, didn't want to watch TV. Maybe she was psychic.

The call came at four. A man was with him in his office, someone who must have come in by way of the rear stairs. It bothered her.

"I'll be there in twenty minutes."

"Okay," she said softly. Not like her to give in so easily.

They closed early on Saturday, I knew. She'd be alone unless she left with the other personnel, which she flatly refused to do. Stubborn.

Halfway there, another call.

"They're fighting!"

"Get out, now."

"I will. I'll be downstairs in the front."

It was very hard not to violate the speed laws, except I didn't want to risk being pulled over, getting delayed. But I pushed it.

She wasn't in the front. I bounded the stairs; the door was locked. I pounded, no response. I yelled. I ran down and around to the rear of the building, up the stairs. The door was ajar. I entered, yelling for her. I went to

Carl's office. He was on the floor. I ran to the front.
Empty, so I went back to Carl.

There was a lot of blood on the floor. He'd been
stabbed, from the looks of his clothing. I checked his
pulse, which I wasn't sure how to do, but felt nothing. I
was panicking, trying to resist it. I started for my
phone, in my car, but realized I could call from there, so
I used the one on her desk. What was her number? It was
in my phone; I couldn't remember it, in my condition, so I
ran downstairs to my car.

Somehow I managed to push the speed dial. It rang.
It rang. And she answered.

"Hello. Ed?"

"Yes, it's me. Where are you?"

"I'm following him."

"Who?"

"It's Bo. I'm on the 101."

"Don't follow him."

"I have to. I saw him leaving. He was hurrying."

"You were in the back?"

"No, I saw his car. He was coming from the alley."

"Don't follow him."

"Why not? Oh! Is Carl alright?"

"He's dead."

"This is it, then. Don't worry, I'll be careful."

I started to scream at her, but caught myself. It was useless. "Which way are you heading?"

"North. We're past Sepulveda."

"Okay. Listen. I'll try to reach Figari. If not, I'll call 911 and report the body. You--"

"Was he stabbed?"

"Uh-huh. Don't get too close. If you lose him, you lose him."

"I won't lose him. He's going fast, though."

I couldn't reach Figari. The weekend. I left a message for him to call me, an emergency. I dialed 911, but hung up. For all I knew they could track me, could stop me. No way. Had to get to Aracely. People had noticed me running on the street, anyway. Carl would be found.

The fast lane all the way. At Sepulveda I called her again.

"Hi. Are you behind me?"

"Yes. Relax. Drive carefully."

"I am, honey. But he's really moving."

"So am I. Where are you?"

"Kanan Road. Past Kanan."

"You know where he's going, don't you?"

"No."

"To the house. To clean up evidence or something, now that he killed Carl."

"Maybe so."

I couldn't catch her. If I was too reckless, had an accident, I'd be of no help. If I got pulled over, perhaps the police would agree to pursue, but most likely not. Sure, they had helicopters, but if they thought I was crazy they'd detain me and not go after them.

I nearly did get into an accident, swerving in and out of lanes. I called her halfway there, she said to stop calling, it was too hard to drive!

"Just wait for me if he goes to the house. Don't let him see you."

"Okay. 'Bye."

I could call 911 and tell them everything, tell them to go to the house. But I didn't know the address, I only knew the way. And what if he wasn't going there? And why would they take my word for it?

Thank God I had gas. Thank you, Jesus.

She's brave, I had to hand it to her.

So Bo did it. He must have wanted to take over the 'business,' but they wouldn't go for it. They said no, he flipped out. Son-of-a-bitch, those young girls. Can't say I felt too sorry for Carl, though.

Get out of my way! Go ahead and honk.

By Ventura, it was growing dark. I had to call. No answer.

Is this the right way? Yes, yes. Which turn? This? Yes, yes.

I saw the house. I saw her car, the door open. Empty. Tried not to screech to a halt, not to slam my door. Had to surprise him.

No lights in the house, but I knew where I was going: the garage. Tripped and fell. Couldn't slow down. The side door was unlocked. It was dark in there, but I found my way to the back room. The door was closed, but I opened it and heard Aracely moaning, or crying. Then I saw them.

She was naked, her hands and ankles tied from behind, tape over her mouth. He was adding a blindfold when he looked up. I started to yell at him but he turned, a wild look in his eyes, and picked up a long knife. As he advanced on me, I yanked out my .38 and shot him. Twice.

THE LOOK OF LOVE

"Can't you close that book and talk to me?"

"What about?"

"Can't you, please?"

"Not if you refuse to tell me what it is!"

"That's mean. I want to talk, for a change."

"About him?"

She paused, tempted to lie. But then said "Yes."

"Forget it. He'll kill me if he hears --"

"Will not! That's stupid. His threats are without a basis in reality, I'm telling you."

"Maybe." He closed the book. "Maybe not. From all you've said --"

"Whatever I've said is between us. He can't know."

"Right, or he'll explode and kill me."

"Baby!"

"Is that an accusation or an endearment?"

Tears came, she had to sit in a chair. The phone rang. Neither of them cared to answer it.

"I'm sorry," he said. The book felt heavy -- he wanted to open it again. Saroyan.

She closed her eyes, the tears slid down her cheeks.

"Every time you tell me something he did, you --" Phil held his tongue, with difficulty. She wouldn't look at him. Her fingers whipped the tears.

Finally she said: "I have to tell someone. He's cruel."

"Then don't marry him." He opened the book, but she took that moment to look, so he closed it again. "It's not my business. I only go by what you say."

"I'm lying? Is that -- ?"

"No, but possibly you're exaggerating."

More tears. "Sure, possibly. I could be crazy. Like he didn't say you were a good friend for me to have, that his work kept him from spending enough time with me, that he <u>liked</u> us hanging out, that --"

"Not that stuff. The other stuff."

"What?" She stared blankly at Phil as if she had no memory of any of it.

"Mistreating you! Bullying you! Threatening you! Pushing you against the car that time, yelling that he'd --"

"Oh! Stop it." She stood up, angry. "You want to think I made it up, think it."

"Not to mention he'd get me if we did anything."

"We already did." She left the room.

"Not everything. Just..." Phil gave up. But he remembered the time in his car when she sucked so hard it hurt.

Later Marilyn left for her place. They kissed when they parted. She squeezed his butt, so he squeezed hers. Of course he wanted to have real sex with her, but she was almost engaged. And he didn't, in his heart, want to mess up her relationship -- and he didn't know the other guy that well. Perhaps she was exaggerating. Perhaps he wasn't that bad. Perhaps he hadn't forced her to participate in a threesome with a prostitute. Who knew? Perhaps it was just a fantasy.

After Marilyn left he worried what she was telling him. Dangerous. Maybe Phil's remarks, in response to the stories of mistreatment, came out more extreme in the telling. Maybe her boyfriend thought the worst -- that Phil was attempting to interfere.

He wasn't, really. Yeah, tell that to the coroner as he takes you to that autopsy surgeon in the middle of the night.

He locked the door, shut the blinds, checked his gun in the drawer, got a beer from the fridge, turned off a couple of lights, sat alone in the living room and drank.

She was so sweet sometimes. He <u>did</u> feel sorry for her. But she loved the guy. No question. Let them marry. So what -- what difference did it make? But Phil had to admit -- as he'd informed her once -- he loved her. Crazy as she was. That look in her face when they talked, when she revealed her inner self to him, trustingly. It was love, too, but she wouldn't, hadn't, didn't express it in words.

What was he doing? Who was the crazy one?

Morning light came through the blinds as Phil crossed from his bedroom, peeking out. No ominous car on the street, no rifle pointed toward his house. What had she told Ron last night on the phone? Of course they would have talked. Maybe he'll order her never to see him again, maybe Phil would be free from it all. Good.

Coffee. Cereal. Misgivings. He checked the message. His brother in Sacramento. What's up, dude? Getting any?

Not hardly. He forced himself to return the call, but fortunately no one answered. His brother and his wife would already be in church.

Oh, that face! Never to see it again? Those breasts, which she teased him with, rarely allowed him to hold, never to touch again? Better this way, he thought. Absolutely better. Stay out of it. Keep away from her.

But those lips! And, yes, that quick mind, those penetrating thoughts, that intellectual power she tried to hide. Never to experience those qualities <u>ever again</u>?

Better this way, yes. Safer.

By afternoon he'd finished the book. It was oddly disappointing. Saroyan left things out -- significant things, like what did it all mean? The reader was required to grasp meaning out of life's little details. But aren't all books, except non-fiction, that way?

The phone didn't ring all day. He tried to call her, but hung up after he'd pushed the speed dial. Marilyn, Marilyn, where are you? With him? Waiting alone, for me to call?

The following morning, Monday, he went to work. Nobody seemed to notice what he was going through. The boss gave him a few instructions; he spent the day re-editing the documentary: Chinese Restaurants Around The Country. Someone else had all the fun filming it, Phil sat in the studio making cuts and trims on the computer. Big Hollywood enterprise. Something to sell to cable. His suggestion to make a documentary about professional wrestlers had been rejected. Then he suggested they call Discovery Channel to see if they'd be interested. The boss conceded he'd think about it.

There was a message on his home phone when he got in. From her.

"Sorry I couldn't call you at work -- I'm nervous to. Please, are you mad at me?"

So much for the better way out. He called. She was there. "Hey, honey. How are you?"

"Fine. But Ron came by in the middle of the night, knocking on my kitchen door. Scared the shit out of me."

"And?"

"And, it was fine. He was nice. Just wanted to see me."

"Good."

"Uh-huh. Are you mad at me?"

"No, I'm not."

"Then say something! You sound -- put-offish."

"Sorry. Did he stay long?"

She laughed. He could picture that face. "He stayed a little while. He was nice."

"You said that already."

"Want to know what we did?"

"Un-uh, no thank you." She laughed again.

"What are you doing?" she asked.

"Playing with myself."

"Nasty boy. How does it feel?"

"Not as good as you doing it." She seemed as though she was purring.

"Don't get me started," she purred.

"Okay. Isn't it smart we don't see each other anymore? Not that I don't want to. But... what's smart here?"

"Not not seeing each other. Can't you take it anymore?"

"I can take it, but... is he still talking about marriage?"

"Yes, so? We're friends."

"Yes, we're friends. But we're so close. You know. Kind of too close, and you're in a bad spot, and --"

"I don't care."

"Marilyn, you must."

"I love the way you say my name."

"Stop. The point is, this is weird. I told you I loved you. How do you feel?"

"I... it's obvious. Isn't it?"

"You... do?"

"I can't help it."

"See? See? It can't work. We --"

"No, I know that. I'm not stupid."

"A bit of a choice needs to be made, Marilyn. Do you want me to make it?"

"No! We can't make a choice. It's too complicated."

"No it isn't. It's simple, really simple. You love him, you want to marry him. Right?"

"That's -- right."

"There's the choice. You've made it."

"I suppose I have."

JUST ANOTHER DAY

Frank stole two cars when he was a teenager. Didn't even have a driver's license yet. Just joy-riding, and he blamed it on Petey, his friend who had had the idea. Stealing them was easy -- Petey knew one old car didn't even need a key to start it, and they got the key for the other one out of the kitchen of the owner. "Everyone was neighbors," Frank told the judge. They'd brought the cars back after a half-hour of fun. But the hard-assed judge didn't care much. Petey and Frank had gone to Juvie. Bleak place, other teenage offenders. Nearly flunked out of high school after missing so much time.

What ever happened to his buddy Petey? Frank had not gotten into any more trouble with the law -- not even drug charges. Sometimes he thought about being in Juvenile Hall, and thought about those poor slobs who were in prison around the country, eating bad food and fighting off rapists. Well, he'd escaped that fate, thank God. Now Frank was idling, watching the dumb news on TV, drinking coffee, calling his friends, waiting for the check from the Screen Actors Guild to come in the mail. Retired at fifty-six. Fuck it. Maybe his agent could find him another job, maybe not. Most of the good parts are for guys in their twenties. He had played a horse trainer on a cable channel movie two years back, for scale. They hadn't cared he had a limp, though most casting agents don't like it. Dumb people. It's a character element! So he limps?

Frank sighed, rose from his chair, clicked off the TV, put water on the stove for more coffee, went into the bathroom to look at his face. Not a bad face. Why won't they hire me? Two of his parts had been in made-for-television movies that had ended up in the top fifteen for the weeks they were on. No series, though. That's where the money is.

His phone rang, for a change. But Frank didn't want to answer it. Bob, a guy he met a long time ago who worked for the fire department as an ambulance driver -- didn't want to talk to him. It would just be the same old shit. Dating anyone? No. Seen any good movies? No. Heard from Millie? No. Want to go to lunch on my day off? Yes, and they would, and talk about the government and the world and girls and movies.

Of course he could call Millie, but she was doing a musical downtown and didn't want to see him anymore, anyway. She'd only be nice and decline to go out with him.

Even the woman at the drive-by window at Carl's Jr. had declined to go out with him. And she'd seemed to like him, too, every time he went through. Guess she didn't like him that much. Or was she waiting for him to ask her a second time? Could be. Guess I'll do that, he thought, as he poured water into a cup, mixing it with instant coffee.

He listened to Bob's message. Same old shit, with a slight variation. Bob had a girlfriend. Great.

Frank opened his front door to look at the trees in the patio. He could hear the machines going in the laundry room. Seemed like that's all his neighbors did was laundry, and talk on their cell phones.

He looked up at the sky. When was Jesus coming back, anyway? To take him away? Not today, he guessed.

Frank closed the door, looked at the poster of Marilyn Monroe on the wall, and then at the poster of Humphrey Bogart. Wouldn't it be cool to be in a movie like the ones they had made? A comedy or a drama -- he didn't care. Just... something.

DASHER

She didn't speak at all when first given the news. Metaphorically her heart sank, and the muscles in her neck tightened. Both hands gripped the messenger's upper arms -- he suspected she wanted "to kill the messenger," yet her grip relaxed, and she closed her baby blue eyes and put her hands to her face.

He, of course, hugged her to offer comfort, and she accepted it passively. The dog sniffed at his feet and looked up at his master in the messenger's arms.

"Sorry" was the only appropriate word. Tragic news depressed all, even when the facts concerned, mainly, the hearer. Mike released his hold, stepping back, a rush of uncomfortable helplessness passing up and down his entire body. Miss Coco looked frail, thinner than ever before, and dropped her hands from her pale face, looking rather intently at the dog. Still she didn't speak.

"It's for the best, I'm sure," Mike said, wishing he hadn't. But rather than slap him she smiled, staring now at him, her blue eyes painful wet orbs that closed immediately. She knelt beside the tiny white dog and said at last:

"Peppy, Dasher is gone. Gone for good." She picked up her confused mutt, stood, smiled again at Mike, said: "Thank you," walked to the chair and sat. "It's alright," she whispered to Peppy. "We'll be fine. I love you." The dog licked her, looked at Mike, and squirmed in his master's lap.

Mike wanted to leave, but yet... she may need something, if only his presence. When a moment passed and she remained silent he stepped backward again.

"Guess I'll go. You gonna be okay?"

She nodded, petting the white dog.

"Don't want me to get you a drink or -- something from the store?"

She merely shook her head, so he stepped back again, touching the door with his fingers. Miss Coco wasn't breathing hard, she wasn't crying anymore. Her head rested on the top edge of the chair. When Mike turned to go the dog jumped from her lap to send him off. Mike stooped to pet him, and went out, closing the door.

She weathered it fairly well. Miss Coco buried her dog in the yard, illegally, and resorted more often than usual to her office. Mike kept out of her way as much as he could. His room was on the second floor. The only other renter worked long hours, came in quite late, and used the kitchen infrequently. Miss Coco had once told him the gentleman had a good job, and was, in her words, "salting it away." Mike rarely saw him. He hope someday he too would have a good job and "salt it away," go on vacation in Hawaii and fall in love with a sexy hula dancer.

For now he wrote his novel and studied his correspondence course -- "Psychology." He mailed in the assignments.

But, naturally, murder was in his heart. The dog killer lived down the street, a few houses away. Mike walked past the place on his way to the grocery store, gritting his teeth and planning a method to kill him. The man was free, had escaped prosecution, had lied to the police, had resumed his odious existence like nothing had happened, like he'd not shot a harmless Cocker Spaniel in his back yard with a rifle.

"Didn't know what it was. Thought maybe it was a burglar. Been burgled before. Made a police report last year. You look and see," Mike had heard him tell the police.

Miss Coco drank brandy, by the fireplace in the lounge, at night. Mike heard her talking on the telephone to her sister, and changing the television channels.

His novel took a nasty turn, the lead character breaking up with his girlfriend, quitting college and joining the Army. But Mike didn't know how to write about Army life, so he stole some things out of *FROM HERE TO ETERNITY*.

The killer lived peaceably, free, down the street. One day, Mike told himself, one day I'll get you. That loving dog, friendly to everyone in this neighborhood! But the man in the house had chased him twice from his front yard, yelling and screaming. <u>That</u> Mike had witnessed from his window. There was no question the man had shot 'Dasher' on purpose, fully aware of who the dog was. Miss Coco wouldn't believe it -- but she was a sweet, middle-aged landlady. Mike saw it differently. And the dog had suffered for days, before succumbing.

Then an idea hit with tidal wave energy. Bash him on the head from behind, run away, hide the rock, sneak to my room, wash my hands, get into bed, let someone find the dog killer, dead. It could never be connected to him. Miss Coco surely wouldn't be blamed. The creep probably had made enemies in his past; the cops would never solve it, no one would care in the least.

The dog killer went to a bar, a few blocks away, a few nights a week. Mike would wait in the bushes, jump out after he passed by on the sidewalk, pop him on the head with great force, and run. Normally their side street was empty that time of night.

He picked his night. He'd sent off the last correspondence lesson, only the final examination remained. There would be less stress that way.

Saturday night was too busy, so Mike chose a week night. Thursday night -- he'd seen the murderer go to the bar on many Thursdays.

He slipped out by the rear stairs. It was after midnight. He got the rock he'd selected from behind the lemon trees, walked secretly around a couple of homes, stationed himself in the bushes near the sidewalk, and waited.

Sweat sprang uncontrollably from his pores, and his breathing was rapid. He calmed himself by visualizing the beach. Only three or four cars went by in, perhaps, twenty minutes.

His throat was dry and Mike wished he'd brought water. Had he really been in the Army he'd have prepared for this. But, of course, a water bottle was one more loose item to think about. Cops are smart. Except they'd believed the dog killer's phony excuse.

Finally the murderer's steps could be heard at the end of the street. They proceeded toward Mike's hideout. The rock felt good in his hands. He shifted it to his right one, braced himself, making sure the dog killer couldn't see him.

The murderer passed by. Mike inched forward. He crouched at the edge of the bushes, he sprang onto the sidewalk, he stepped silently, in tennis shoes, to the man, he raised the rock, he moved closer to strike.

The problem was, unfortunately, he couldn't do it. His arm froze in mid-air, his sneaking run stopped, the man kept walking. The chance had passed. Blood rushed, pulsed, in Mike's head like Niagara Falls. Damn! He wanted to throw the rock at the man's head, the murderer's head, but he didn't. He wanted to yell a profanity, but he didn't. The man walked on. Mike could run after him, probably bash his head in, even now. But he didn't.

He returned to his room after discarding the useless rock, and washed his hands. Mike sat on his bed and felt how sticky and wet his shirt was. And he knew he could not, could never, do it. There was a difference between him and a dog killer.

A MYSTERIOUS TRIP

What I wanted was a chocolate shake, without whipped cream, to go. "Para llevar," I told the cashier, guessing from her looks that she spoke Spanish -- espanol. But --

"What?"

"To go. ¿No habla usted espanol?"

She laughed the tiniest fraction. "Some... except..."

"You don't understand? Yo quiero para llevar."

A little more of a laugh. "But... your accent!"

Oh, great. "So I have an accent? Impossible!"

"Yes," was all she said. No laugh.

Finally someone prepared my shake while I waited near the door, as various people came in and were seated. I was impressed by the efficiency. "How many?" "This way, please."

I got my shake. The cashier took the money, gave me my change, told me to watch out it didn't spill. "Okay. Adiós."

She giggled a tiny bit more. "Adiós."

Outside in the hot sun I walked morosely to my car in the lot. Can't even impress a dark-haired Los Angeles cashier. Fine.

At my car I pushed the remote on my key chain and dared a sip of the shake. Don't spill it! Like I'm going to? As I opened my door, making damn sure I didn't spill any, I put the large cup on the console and sat down. I heard a man's raised voice and looked through the rearview mirror to see the manager, probably, who had been inside, walking with _my_ cashier. He'd been frowning, I'd noticed, from a few paces to the left of her, when I'd said "Adiós." Not unusual. Male co-workers generally disliked my feeble flirting attempts with female cashiers. In fact, it had happened only two days previously at the car wash, and then the guy had given me a tough time -- tougher than called for -- over the fact I tried to pay with American Express. How absurd of me! Why, they only took Visa and Master Card! But I knew what he was doing -- attempting to look better than me in front of the cashier, whom he was most likely interested in, trying to take out on a date.

But now my reminiscing was cut short. I heard a female voice uplifted in protest. Looking around I saw the manager and cashier near the corner of the restaurant, in front of a car, arguing. He stepped toward her and slapped her hard. She ducked, late, and turned away.

<u>Do not get involved</u>. Let it go. Domestic disputes, etc., are none of -- but he raised his hand once more. She saw it and bravely hollered at him to stop.

Naturally I got out, watching, ready to... what? Rather than strike this time, he lowered his hand and pushed at her, saying something I couldn't hear. Two customers entered the restaurant door, appearing not to notice. I walked over.

"Make up your mind, you stupid bitch," he yelled, and slapped her again. She kicked him in the leg and fell back, and I grabbed his shoulder when he lunged at her. He spun like a cat to see who I was, and threw a punch. I ducked, not fast or far enough, but it bounced off the top of my head.

"Who are you? Get out of this!"

For an instant there were no more punches, so I asked: "What's your problem? I saw you slap her, that's all."

It in fact pacified him, but he was looking me over. Bigger than him. Taller.

"Never mind. She's alright."

"Are you?" I asked her.

"No!" She kicked at him again.

"Ouch!" I wanted to laugh when he said it, but he grabbed at her, so... I had to do something. I pushed at his shoulder to ruin his balance, and braced for another punch, which came in an instant.

Blocking it, I hit him in the face with a hard jab, slapped <u>him</u> this time, and moved between the two of them.

"I'll kill you if I ever see you again," he rumbled as he walked back to the front door.

She clutched my arm, which made it all worthwhile. She also yelled a nasty Spanish word, which I hadn't ever cared to learn (but had nonetheless), at his retreating figure. The man entered the restaurant without looking at us.

She wouldn't let go of me, which was okay, but I'd gotten into something now. Not my style. How she trembled! Alright in bed, but not here.

"You're sure you're okay?"

Trembling, but with an angry face, my cashier whispered: "Probably you saved me."

"Are you hurt?" I looked at her cheek. Red, but unmarked. "What was that about?"

No answer, and she released her grip. I looked to the front door. A family was entering. No manager coming out

with a burly cook. My cashier was trembling less, yet
there was this intense rain cloud -- fear -- in her eyes.
I stood quietly until she whispered: "Thank you, amigo.
Did you get hurt or anything?"

"No. What are you going to do?"

"I don't have a car. Felix was my ride." That little
laugh. "No ride. I'm off work." She gave me that look
women do, that smile.

"My pleasure. Give you a lift if you want." She
broadened the smile, like they do, when you provide them
their wishes.

"Are you sure? What's your name?"

"Uh, Patrick, but call me amigo. I like it." I
pointed to the front door. "That's Felix?"

"Uh-huh." She said that bad word again.

Halfway to her brother's house in Malibu, upper
Malibu, my cashier cried a little bit, comparable to her
tiny laugh. Her body was tiny, also, I noticed -- but not
<u>too</u> tiny. Just petite. Not like that French neighbor I
once had. <u>That</u> was a small woman. Had to carry her
clothes basket to the laundry on the corner for her,
occasionally.

Her brother would put her up, my cashier said. She was afraid to go home.

"Do you live with Felix?"

"No! But he knows where it is. He could go there. I don't care to --"

"I understand," I interrupted. Didn't want to hear about it. Just wanted to drop her off, get going. Too much trouble.

We were almost to Zuma Beach. The sky was lovely -- rain coming. Left turn off Pacific Coast Highway, a small house among others, not near enough to the beach for a view, but very pleasant. Down a kind of alley between another row of homes, I parked.

"What's your name, by the way?"

"Eve." She smiled.

"That's not Latina."

"Who said I was? You. Not me." Her laugh.

We got out and she rang the bell and I wanted to leave but then again she may be in trouble, so I stayed. Good thing, too. No one there.

It was getting dark, cold, rain on the way, a girl named Eve, an empty house, a crazy manager. A violent, crazy manager.

"Eve what?"

"Militis."

"Huh?" She laughed. Then she got a key from a plastic envelope in a hanging plant and opened the door, waving me in. I went.

Eve turned on the lights. Well-furnished, not beachy. She closed the door.

"Where's your brother?"

She only shrugged and opened the refrigerator in the kitchen. After a moment she asked: "Hungry?"

It surprised me, and I said no. I'd finished the shake during the drive. She hadn't wanted any.

"I am." Her hands went to work, the microwave hummed, a bowl of noodles and vegetables resulted. "Drink, amigo?"

Why was I nervous? This was _sort_ of a wonderful event, possibly leading to sex. "Just water, thanks."

Eve insisted I sit in the living room and soon we were there, her eating, me drinking water in a strange glass, raindrops landing on the pavement outside. My mind jumped forward to her asking me to stay. The whole night. No Felix, no brother.

"Want some grass?"

"No, no. Thanks."

"Okay. I don't either."

"Go ahead if --"

"No, I don't. It's only my brother does."

"Okay. Where do you suppose he is?"

"Could be out of town." She stood up. "I'll look."
She left for an upstairs area, bedrooms, I guessed. Weird
idea I had: she'd find a dead body.

But no, she returned, saying: "Yep, he's gone. I can
see a suitcase and clothes are missing."

"All of them?"

"No," she laughed. "Only a few items, silly!" She
sat to eat the rest of the food in the bowl. She was
feeling okay now. Time to head out, I figured.

"Hey, amigo, will you do me a favor?"

"Sure. What?"

"Will you spend the night? I'm afraid."

I kept a poker face. "Why, certainly. I don't mind."

She laughed. "Men are so bad."

"Not me. I <u>was</u> bad, but I got divorced."

A second passed before she laughed again. I joined in
to assure her I was only joking. Doubt if it worked.

"Anyway, I really can't stay here alone. I don't mean Felix will show up, or like that. I just can't take the idea of --"

"I understand. Don't sweat it."

"Only..."

"What?"

She stared at me. "I don't really know you. You saved me, but... excuse me. That's crappy."

"It's alright, I'm not a bad person."

"Of course you aren't."

"I can sleep here," I said, pointing to the couch. "You're safe, believe me."

She laughed. "You don't have to sleep on the couch."

That's what I wanted to hear.

It turned out to be a good night, and we both slept well (or at least I thought we did), although Eve was on the computer when I woke up. I gave her a hug from behind and went to take a shower. When I came out she was not there -- presumably in the kitchen making breakfast.

But she was not. She was gone. Fled. I wandered through the house, growling. No note. No breakfast. Then I ran to the door to pull it open to check on my car. It was there, of course. Eve wouldn't be a car thief. But where had she gone? To walk on the beach?

I dressed and made coffee and waited, increasingly uncomfortable in a stranger's house. Correction, <u>I</u> was the stranger in her <u>brother's</u> house. I also worried that I'd had no condom, had relied trustingly on Eve's assurance she took the pill. But so few women used that anymore, I wondered if I'd made an error in judgment. Tempted to peek into desk drawers and rifle papers, I strolled around, evaluating this man's existence. Difficult to know his work; the place looked nondescript, impersonal. Nothing characteristic in the way of clothes: a few suits, jogging stuff, plain dress shoes, no woman's apparel. I left.

After breakfast at the Malibu Inn, my conscience began to bother me. Perhaps she'd arranged to meet Felix somewhere to discuss their problem, and he'd done away with her. Seriously. She wouldn't have wanted to tell me where she was going. Could have walked to the gas station, or the market near PCH and met him, rode off with him to a secluded spot, been strangled and tossed in the woods. Sure. I drove past the house for good measure. Nothing. I drove through the nearby market area. Nothing.

There was only one thing to do -- go to the restaurant. If Felix wanted to get into a fight, there was nothing I could do about it. If he was an ex-con and stuck me with a shiv, that's just the way it would go. I didn't have much to live for anyway. A few thousand bucks in the bank, income from the farm my folks had left me. A sister in San Francisco who couldn't care less, the way she never wrote after her last scathing letter denouncing my lifestyle. Not that I had one. That was her grievance, I suppose. Was it my fault I got divorced and got fired and quit looking for another job? Was it? Yes.

At the restaurant I grew nervous in spite of my profound history of never being nervous in response to threatening situations. Inside, the manager saw me. I signaled for him to come over. He did, not smiling.

"What can I do for you?" he asked.

"Remember, I had the confrontation with you out back yesterday?" I smiled.

"Sure I remember -- so?"

"The girl, Eve. Have you seen her?"

"What business is it of yours?"

"None, I suppose. Only -- is she around?"

"Take a look." He started to walk away, which I should have allowed him to do, but it's not in my nature.

"Be nice and tell me where she is."

Of course that stopped him, but when he turned I saw he was not angry.

"Pal, I haven't the faintest idea. She didn't show up for work. Anything else?"

"No. Thanks."

Felix gave a lopsided grin, and turned away.

I let him go, this time, no knife in my gut. Outside I sat in my car, thinking. She wasn't there. Let it go. If the manager was lying he was too adept at it for me to cope with. I called a friend, John, a good friend, who took the time to listen to everything, and offered this advice:

"The broad slipped out on you. So what? You know how women are. Drop it. Or did she get under your skin?"

"Kind of."

"Then leave a note at the brother's. I don't recommend you go to the manager again."

"No, right. Okay. I'll do that. Thanks."

I left a note taped to the door. It had stopped raining, so with luck it would be there if he showed up. When he showed up. Or if she showed up.

Eve was too petite for me. Like having sex with a big soft bird. She did come, though. That was unusual, for me. Not a long-laster.

By evening the following day I had curiously forgotten about it, but she called.

"Hello, amigo."

"Eve! Where --? Are you okay?"

"Yes, but --"

"Where are you?!"

"In Long Beach at my mother's."

"You're kidding. I -- I was worried about you. You left, you --"

"I had to. I can't explain it now."

"Well, try."

"I can, but not now."

"Did you get my note?"

"My brother called me."

"Do you have a cell phone?"

"Not with me. In my apartment."

"Supposed to carry the cell phone with you, have a regular phone in your apartment."

"I know," she giggled a tiny bit.

"Have you gone back there? What happened?"

"No, and I'll tell you later."

"I want to see you."

"Dangerous."

"For you or for me?"

"For you, actually. But if you truly want to see me, I'll meet you at Grinders." She gave me the directions. Another restaurant. Guess her mother wasn't supposed to be involved.

On the way to Long Beach I got slightly nervous again. How could this be "dangerous"? Was Felix her boyfriend? He hadn't seemed upset. Illogical. Why didn't she dare return to her apartment? How had she gotten to Long Beach? The only two things I understood were her not going in to work and her not wanting to explain to me over the phone, in someone else's, her mother's, house. My mother had been nosy also.

Fortunately for my self-esteem Eve was there in the restaurant. Café, really, nearly as nice as where she worked. Or had worked.

I sat across from her, feeling awkward. She looked pale.

"Hi, amiga," I said.

"¿Como esta?"

"Bien, but you're not Spanish, remember?"

"Or Latina, or Hispanic, or South American."

I laughed to be nice, embarrassed. I wanted to kiss her for being alive.

We had coffee and sandwiches. She told me everything. Eve had phoned for a cab to pick her up on the street. Not sure I believed her, but it was possible. She had gone to Long Beach. She'd been afraid and hadn't known how to say goodbye. John wouldn't be surprised.

"But what's all the danger?"

"Felix's boss owns another spot in Cabo. San Lucas? You know?"

"I know." At the end of the peninsula. Resort area. Resplendent sea, turistas galore.

She played with her silverware. "There's prostitutes there. You know. Part of the restaurant."

"Okay. Big deal."

"Felix is part of it, goes down there to manage the business a lot. He speaks Spanish."

"Glad someone does."

Those eyes flashed like dark gems. "This seems like nothing to you, but... the boss wants me to... go there. To be a hooker."

"Oh. That's it. What for? No, I mean, of course he would. But if you don't want to --"

"I don't want to."

"And Felix insisted?"

"He did. You see, we had an affair."

"You and Felix?"

"Well, a short one."

"Yet he wants you to go to Cabo?"

"Uh-huh. He has no feelings."

Purple, the sky in the west looked to me, as the sun set behind thick rain clouds. Eve's story also seemed dense, dark, and disturbing, because she flat refused to go to the police. Couldn't blame her, yet that was my recommendation. Otherwise she'd remain in constant jeopardy of, she believed, violence and, more likely, verbal abuse. Underneath it glowed an irritating spark of nagging suspicion -- unformulated but there -- that this wasn't all there was to the "story." It struck me Felix had been too calm, and the cab ride without saying goodbye too unbelievable. My ego? Maybe. Felix not knowing what she'd told me might be an explanation for his manner. Or, it could have been the punch in the mouth he'd sustained. Bullies don't care for resistance; they move rapidly to escape it.

I followed her along PCH to an affluent community alcove where I was to watch from a distance while she drove her mother's car through a gate and parked, and safely entered the large house okay. That done, I was to leave, to forget all about her and our experience. Sure. Not being a bully, I had to accept it. I did get a kiss before we left Grinders' parking lot. Little anxious bird kiss.

Up PCH to Malibu, not intending exactly to knock on her brother's door, I proceeded moodily, disliking her wishes but certain she knew much more than I did about this whole situation.

Would talking to her brother be such a bad idea? Only if Eve was lying. In that case, what did I care if I messed things up? He may not know anything. Was it so bad if he knew about this prostitution deal? She'd not asked me <u>not</u> to speak with him. A feeble out, but reasonable. The only out I had.

So I knocked on his door. He didn't open it for a long time -- more than two minutes, it seemed like.

"Hi, I'm Patrick O'Hara, a friend of Eve's. I left the note here yesterday."

"Right. Hello."

"It's -- I only want a minute of your time." When he didn't invite me in, I continued: "Are you aware she's in some sort of trouble?"

"What trouble?"

"At work. The boss is pressuring her to go to Mexico to work, and --"

"How is that trouble?"

"They are insisting."

He laughed. "I'll call her. Can't be but so hard to say no, can it?"

"Well, she made it sound like they were very insistent. It's not really any of my business, but she's a nice girl, and I don't like their pushing her around, you know what I mean?"

"I do know what you mean. I'll call her. Anything else?"

"No."

"Alright. Would you give me -- oh, never mind, your phone number's on the note, isn't it? Good number for you?" As I nodded he laughed again. "Very nice of you to care."

"Seemed important."

"Maybe. I'll let you know, if you wish."

"Thanks."

One thing, just one thing was wrong, I realized as I drove away. A tiny thing, yes, but... no, two things. First, he'd not offered his name, at the start, which I suppose was acceptable, but, second, he'd not asked if she'd called me as per my note. An obvious question, since he'd passed it on to her. At the least he might have told me he had, when I mentioned it. Or... since he didn't know me, possibly he was just being protective. Yeah, amigo, you're over-analyzing this deal. The man was only being careful.

Too careful -- that's what bothered me. And if he knew what I knew, he'd never laugh it off like that. And if he was faking nonchalance, what for? That I didn't like.

It rained once more -- those clouds were moving over the city. I sat in my apartment, forcing time to pass before calling her. The number was in my phone, luckily not "restricted." At eight I called.

"Hello?"

"Eve? It's Patrick."

"Hi."

"Sorry to bother you. How's everything?"

"Good. You're not bothering me. I'm glad you called."

"Great. I thought maybe I shouldn't, but I want to see you again. I --"

"Do you?"

"Don't act so surprised." She laughed a bit. "The way we left it, I couldn't tell if you were okay with that, or what."

"I know."

"Anyway, let's go out. What are you doing?"

"I'm..."

"What?"

"I went shopping. I'm packing. Want to go to Cabo?"

"No. Are you joking?"

"Not joking. Want to go?"

"Please explain. But, yes, I'll go."

"Cool. I can't explain now, but I will. You know.
I'm leaving at midnight. Can you make it?"

A subtle chill ran over my body. "At midnight? From
the airport? Or are you -- ?"

"On a yacht. From Wilmington. Pier 23. I'll meet
you. But get there by twenty of, okay? Oh, the boat's the
'Jinx.'"

"You must be kidding."

"No, amigo. It's all true. I'll explain."

"But -- how many days?"

"About a week. Have a passport?"

"I have."

A week in Cabo? Or more accurately, a few days, minus
travel time. A yacht? I parked in the lot at Pier 23,
took the ticket, carried my two bags to the dock, searched
vainly until I remembered yachts don't have sails like the
old days.

A large ship, the 'Jinx.' Nearly a cruise ship. No
customs -- that would be in Cabo. I didn't see her when I

boarded but was expected, shown to my tiny cabin, led to the aft deck where she was waiting, alone, and when she stood, embraced her.

"Amigo!"

"How mysterious you are."

"Me? Sit down. Thirsty?"

I nodded, sitting at the table with her. A uniformed crew member made me a vodka on the rocks. Eve was sipping a dark beer.

"Come on, tell me. The suspense is killing me."

"Don't! You shouldn't say that!"

"Easy. Just a figure of speech."

"Bad, amigo. You shouldn't put that out into the universe. Take it back."

"Okay, the suspense is <u>not</u> killing me."

By the time we were heading out, rocking suddenly toward open sea, Wilmington fading from view, the cold air biting a bit too much, Eve had recounted another difficult-to-believe story. She was not going to sell sexual favors to the restaurant's clientele, she was not being abducted by the boss. She was, in fact, taking a vacation.

"Whose ship is this?"

"A couple, a wonderful retired couple who used to eat at the restaurant often."

"Are they here?"

"Certainly -- but they're in bed now."

"Of course."

"Captain and Mrs. Hunt. You'll like them. He was in the oil business, but sold it all to travel the world."

"The Hunts? From Texas?"

"Oh, distantly related to them. But almost as wealthy."

"Just how wealthy?"

She shrugged. "Say, you look funny. Something wrong?"

"Kind of. Isn't Cabo where you didn't care to go?"

"Yes, yes. It's all a coincidence. They happened, by accident, to be going there on a short trip, and invited me. Said I could bring a companion."

"Nice. Separate accommodations?"

She giggled. "What could I say?"

"Right. Hey, tell me, aren't you afraid to run into the boss down there?"

"No, I'll avoid his part of town."

We didn't stay up much later. Eve let me kiss her at her cabin, but without an invitation to enter. I was very tired, anyway. We'd meet for breakfast in the morning. I slept well - the rolling induces sleep. But, was I to believe any of this?

Cruising along the coast, smooth blue sea, nippy wind, bright sunlight, tasty eggs, a feeling of well-being tinged with impending doom -- what's not to like? Not to mention sweet anticipation of sexual delight that very night. Eve looked happy, wearing white shorts, sunblock, and a floppy hat. Her bikini top covered enough to make a statement: look if you dare. I dared.

Still no Hunts by 10 o'clock. Eve showed me around the 'Jinx,' introduced me to the crew, laughed when I declined to "take the wheel for a minute, why don't you?" Were they crazy? What if I screwed up or we struck a big swell and I lost control and the 'Jinx' went sideways? No chance, I was told. The pilot was an engaging young gentleman who knew his business, apart from his willingness to let me steer. "Charlie," she called him.

"Come on, I want to show you something," Eve insisted after we left the bridge.

"I've seen it already, but I would like to again."

"What?" She didn't get it, so I played dumb.

"It's in the lounge. Follow me."

The lounge was smaller than I expected, but of course this wasn't a cruise ship. She pointed to photos in a glass case, photos of the Hunts' world travels. One was of Eve, and them, and a forbidding looking bearded man, standing outside a hotel.

"Tahiti! Ever been there?"

"No. Who's that guy with you?"

"My ex. Never mind him."

Drinks at lunch, more rocking, and at last, the Hunts.

"Please don't get up. So nice to meet you." Mrs. Hunt was warm and didn't look old enough to be retired, but Beverly Hills surgeons had a way with rich women, I'd heard. Captain Hunt looked older, but robust.

"Mr. O'Hara. Nice to meet you. Enjoying the voyage?"

"Yes, sir. Thank you for inviting me. This ship is fantastic."

"A home away from home, for us."

We sat for an hour discussing the world, politics, terrorism, weather, global warming, my history, and Eve's needing a new job. From what I gathered, they only knew the manager and she didn't get along, so she'd quit. <u>Of course</u> she'd find a new place, but why she refused the Hunts' offer of assistance remained a mystery to them. Ah, well, she's a fine girl.

The mystery to me was why these people hadn't any other friends aboard. But, not my place to question it. Eve drank too much and excused herself to take a nap.

"The sea makes me so sleepy! 'Bye, honey." I got a kiss on the mouth for just being there.

"We were both glad when she divorced that monster, I don't mind telling you," the Captain said gravely, as Mrs. Hunt nodded. "Patrick, have you considered ethanol?"

"Oh, well," I paused, grasping the line of his thinking: my farm. "Soybeans? Yes, I have. although I was told the cost of producing and transporting ethanol was still too high to --"

"Yes, that's true," the oil man interjected. "For now. But technology can advance quickly."

"I'll keep researching it, if you recommend --"

"I do. Fossil fuels are running out, as I don't doubt you are aware. It's a new world. My generation has just about ruined the environment, and alternative energy, <u>renewable</u> energy, is the future."

This guy was a reformed baron, a friendly, kindly reformed oil baron. The drinks had loosened my tongue to the point I blurted:

"That's great to hear you say, Mr. Hunt. Are there any more oil men like you? I hope so."

"Not so many, my friend. They aren't willing to be realistic. Although"-- he glanced at his wife -- "some of us felt all along we were disserving the world, but... we have to answer to boards and stockholders, you know."

"Yes, I understand."

"We aren't such greedy, bad people as the liberal media makes us out to be."

"No, surely not."

"Are you ready for a stroll, dear?" Mrs. Hunt touched his bare arm. I couldn't tell if the conversation, his revelation to me, had upset her or not.

"Yes, good idea. Just what the doctor ordered." They stood and excused themselves. Creepy how I hadn't been invited. But, then again, I was only a guest of Eve's.

Charlie, the ship's pilot, and, perhaps, Captain -- although Mr. Hunt was referred to as Captain, so the actual ship hierarchy escaped me -- announced via intercom, dinner at 6:00. Or rather, 4 bells. Eve had emerged from her cocoon at 3:00, whereupon we played in the game room and examined the library. The games bored me and the technical industry literature even more so -- with the exception of a complete collection of Zane Grey novels. The author had loved to travel by sea, himself, and wrote a wonderful non-western about Tahiti: *THE REEF GIRL*, which reminded me to question Eve concerning her trip there.

"It's the best spot in the whole world!"

"That explains the mutiny of the 'Bounty.'"

"Mutiny on the Bounty," she corrected.

"I meant the real mutiny, not the movie."

"Which one? There were several."

"I meant the actual... hey, you're putting me on."

"Me? Yeah, I would like to put you on."

"Hmm. Tonight?"

"If you aren't too tired." She put her fingers to my cheek. "Or bored."

"'Spect I can manage to stay awake."

"We'll see." She turned to exit the library, which was only one row deep, and I followed her. The ship lurched hard, putting us both against the bulkhead, and I took the opportunity to encircle her waist with my arm. The ship lurched again, and Eve looked frightened. We heard hollering from above, but then all was calm and quiet.

"Strange," she said. "Wonder what happened?"

We took the passageway to a staircase and went up. A crew member stood outside the wheelhouse facing us.

"Are you two alright?"

"Yes. What happened?" I asked as we approached.

"A boat ran across our bow twice. Just joy-riding, I guess. Please, you can't go in now."

"Why not?" Eve asked quickly.

"Captain Hunt gave orders. Why don't you go to your cabins?" Before she objected he added: "In case they try it again."

"Was it very close?"

"Yes, sir. Close enough. We had to turn twice. I'm sure you noticed."

"Let's go to our cabins." Eve pulled my arm.

"I don't want to," I told her. "There may be danger.
Pirates."

The crew member laughed at me. "No, sir. Not likely.
Looked like young kids -- college students -- having fun.
Charlie's warned them."

"I heard someone yelling," I remarked. The crew
member leaned forward confidentially:

"Told them: 'If you try that again, you're dead.'"
He laughed and leaned back.

"Seriously?" I pictured a big gun pointed at the
students, firing repeatedly.

"Well, we don't want a shipwreck, do we?"

"No, we don't," Eve replied, pulling at me. Then the
ship changed directions, it felt like, but gently. He
blinked and said: "Excuse me now. Please go to your
cabins. Captain's orders." He slipped inside, leaving us
in no small way astonished.

But, not hearing any gunfire, I complied with the
order that Eve was only too happy to follow. No more
sudden lurching, and we reached her door, which she opened
to reveal a made bed, an uncurtained porthole with glinting
sea outside, and said: "Coming in?"

I did, noting to myself these weren't the exact circumstances I'd planned on for entering her cabin. Nevertheless she flopped on the bed, rolling over invitingly. I took the only chair, beside a very small desk attached to the bulkhead, and exhaled:

"Quite something, don't you think?"

"_Pirates_," she giggled. "You're funny."

"Could happen. _Has_ happened."

"Not around here. I know the incident you're referring to. That was India or somewhere." She adjusted her body once again.

I looked at my watch. She stared at me. When I didn't speak, she flung her floppy hat at her suitcase by my chair, and reached to remove her bikini top, but stopped.

"Shall I?"

"Frankly, I'm not in the mood." That caused more than a giggle. "No offense." I crossed the short space to her bed and sat beside her. "For some reason that so-called 'joy-riding' thing disturbs me. For instance, _two_ bow crossings seems... weird. And Charlie's threat was over the top. 'You'll be dead?'"

"It _was_ dangerous."

"True enough."

Her hands had returned from that bikini-removing effort, and now rested on my leg.

"When do you think you'll be in the mood?"

The dining room wasn't exactly bustling when we arrived at six-o-five. A waiter was attending our hosts at a large table in the center, food had been installed in seaworthy trays on a shelf along the wall, music played from hidden speakers, yet the room looked oddly empty.

Eve and I sat.

"Hello! How are you enjoying yourselves?" Mrs. Hunt politely engaged us, immediately.

"Fine, fine," was my response.

"Another terrific cruise," Eve added.

"Do you like fish? There are several kinds -- take a look," Mrs. Hunt said, pointing to the metal trays, full of far too much.

We ate and drank and small-talked our way to the real subject: the bow-crossers.

"Naughty boys," Mrs. Hunt remarked coldly. "Where did they come from, do you think, dear?"

"Oh, my guess up the coast in San Diego.   Looked to be American.   There was another boat, too, farther away.   Not very large.   Not festive, either."

"Have to be careful of kidnappers," Mrs. Hunt said casually, as though they were field mice.

"Does that happen?" I promptly asked.

"Not often, but it does happen," Mr. Hunt noted gravely.   "But to board us they'd need firepower, overwhelming firepower, which we saw no evidence of."

Eve jumped in: "Have you reported this?   To anyone? The Mexican authorities?"

"Certainly, Eve.   Someone will meet us at Cabo. Nothing will come of it, I'm sure."

"Charlie was yelling at them?"

Mr. Hunt laughed agreeably, "Yes, sir, good old Charlie.   Ex-military."

"Doesn't look hardly old enough," I offered.

"Oh, yes, an officer -- in Iraq."

That stopped the conversation for a brief interval. Finally I spoke up:

"What are your plans in Cabo, if I might ask?"

The couple shrugged simultaneously.

"Shopping," the Captain replied, glancing at his wife. "And visiting friends."

"No scuba diving?" I asked, half-joking.

"Ha! Never! Don't go in the water much."

Mrs. Hunt smiled and asked, "Are you certified, Mr. O'Hara?"

"Please, call me Patrick. I am, Mrs. Hunt, but don't get down much."

"Oh, well, we have all sorts of equipment," Mr. Hunt said. "Don't we, Maggie?" She nodded. "Put it to use if you wish. No need to rent anything."

"Thank you. Eve?"

"Un-uh! I'll snorkel with you, though."

"Alright. Let's do that." I didn't bother asking the Hunts. But I was curious about one more thing: "Shouldn't you have security on shore -- a bodyguard or two?"

"Ha!" Captain Hunt took a sip of his wine. "That's handled. They'll be around, not more than twenty feet away."

"Very good."

"Tell him what you're really doing this trip, Captain. He's alright. He saved me, remember?"

The Captain's eyes met mine, and Mrs. Hunt laughed: "Why, Eve."

"It isn't anything so exciting, but it is a secret," the Captain said, his eyes on me.

"If it's a secret you needn't divulge it."

"Come on, come on. Or I will," Eve giggled.

He shrugged, but this time his wife did not, and he turned his unblinking eyes toward her.

"I'd trust him," she said.

The Captain took more wine, obviously getting his words together... "Let's say long-time associates meet every year to discuss business. At various resorts around the world. But we prefer the press, the media, to keep away. That's all." He looked at me. I stared back. "Over the years we've discovered informal gatherings tend to produce innovative ideas."

"Sounds good to me. You can catch up on what everyone is doing, and learn, possibly, of any problems to be dealt with."

"Exactly, exactly. Smart boy. Of course I wouldn't be able to include you, or Eve."

"Of course. Don't expect it, naturally."

Eve kicked me under the table. I guessed she thought
I was being sarcastic. I wasn't.

In bed we had a good time, a little distracted
nevertheless. What was on her mind Eve never said; what
was on mine centered on this secret annual meeting the
Hunts attended around the globe with other oil men and
captains of industry. What were they doing?

Harmless? Or formulating strategy to screw Third
World populations for the enrichment of a select elite?
Or, worse, devising plans to introduce our military forces
where we (they, the elite) desired greater control over
leaders and natural resources. They'd counter: "Hey, you
all have full gas tanks and groceries and stocked shelves
everywhere -- quit complaining. Want another depression
with high unemployment and scarce supply? No, certainly
you don't. Let us take care of it for you. Relax."

Unfortunately that evening our activity fell short of
major enjoyment, and as I left Eve's cabin my soul ached
for another opportunity. It would come, my mind told my
soul. On my bed I prayed to the loving God I believed in,
a God of omnipotent will and inscrutable plans, a God I

hoped would protect us from the peril my imagination imprecisely perceived.

The morning sky was overcast and gloomy, hinting rain, which sprinkled the 'Jinx' by noon. I stood on deck beneath a raised lifeboat, pondering the threads of thought leading to my feeling of anxiety. Rational? Not by themselves -- threads don't mean much without supporting fabric. And there wasn't any. Yet the dread persisted. Not that I cared, for myself, but Eve and our hosts could be in danger -- somehow I believed that. It wasn't only the so-called joy-riding college kids. It was the mystery of the voyage, Eve's ex-boss's purported sex business, the brother's too subtle behavior, and the specter of her bearded ex-husband. Where was he? Someone -- was it the Captain or Mrs. Hunt? -- had called him a "monster."

At lunch I asked Eve: "How long were you married?"

Without hesitation she replied: "Two years."

"A mistake?"

"No, not really. We had a good relationship, generally. Why?"

"No reason. Well, correct that. I do have a reason. Where is he?"

"Pittsburgh."

"Really? Did you live there?"

"No -- he moved. We lived in L.A. What's your reason?"

"Oh, you know, could he be carrying a torch, trailing you around, plotting to kill us?" I laughed, "Ha-ha."

"Sick puppy."

"Him or me?"

"Thou _and_ he."

"As to me, I deny the charge, but as to him, what's the deal? Bad dude?"

"How does drug trafficking suit you? Not that I knew about it, until he told me."

"Then you divorced him?" She nodded. "Was he ever caught?"

"Not as far as I know. Must we talk about this? He hid it from me. He had a regular job -- designing homes for a contractor. Even had a studio in our house, where he worked often. I saw many of his designs. Didn't suspect a thing, except..."

"Except...?"

"Disturbing-looking friends. You know."

"Of course. And sudden trips?"

"Not many, but, yes. And he didn't sleep well."

"Naturally not."

"Must we?"

"No, no. Forget about him. Think of me only."

The following day we hung out with Mr. and Mrs. Hunt.
They wanted to play bridge, so I admitted I didn't know
how. Eve made a valiant effort to teach me, and by four
o'clock (8 bells) -- I was picking it up. Good to know if
I ever met up with the Hunts again.

They put on a movie -- *CASINO ROYALE*. Popcorn, too.
One crew member joined us. Said he'd read the book, had
loved it. I had, also, a couple of decades ago. Eve shot
me a curious look as I recalled she'd asked me twice how
old I was. Women always want to know, if you look over
thirty, for some reason. Husband hunting? I'd have to
tell her sooner or later. The movie was good. Especially
that actress Eva Green.

Dinner again, small-talk again. Mr. Hunt explained
how a "mystery" ship had passed the sinking "Titanic" in
1912, according to survivors, and kept going. Weird. He
implied a connection to a rival passenger ship line that
had a lot to gain -- "substantially" was the word he used -

- by the Titanic sinking. I supposed he might know about such things.

The sinking ship notion did my pseudo-premonition no good, but Eve's giggling when we turned to more light-hearted conversation restored that sense of well-being sea travel induced. Mrs. Hunt told two off-color jokes, which surprised me, as tame as they were. It seemed inappropriate to tell my usual farmer's daughter one, so I kept quiet. Dessert was very good -- except it had marshmallows in it. Didn't think anyone ate those anymore.

We all sat on the stern in comfortable chairs, discussing the sky, which had finally emerged, and the stars, the vastness of the universe, and the Captain's disinclination to ponder the age-old question: just how far did the universe go, and what, if anything, was beyond? Mrs. Hunt laughed at him, which didn't seem rude the way she did it, and said: "The Captain doesn't like the unknown, but I find it fascinating."

In bed we made up for the night before, but we had to sleep, as we would be pulling into Cabo during the early morning, and must prepare to "check out the town," as Eve put it. So I went to my own room. The beds were too small for two people, anyway, even <u>if</u> one of us was five-foot-three in sandals.

There was a semblance of a customs process on board in the morning, but I could see being rich greased the wheels of foreign travel considerably -- a few questions, a signature, a stamp or two, and Eve and I were in the launch chugging toward shore.

The Hunts were already gone, intent on their secret corporate gathering, presumably. The sky was brilliant, the water peaceful blue-green, the hotel skyline picturesque. Cabo San Lucas, a gem at the southern tip of Baja, beamed romantically. I put my arm around my companion; she snuggled briefly, then took another photo of Cabo.

Refusing the several offers of mini-tours and excursions, we walked to town -- a few blocks -- and wandered past shops, restaurants, and information booths. Eve was happy, so I was happy. Street peddlers offered silver bracelets for sale, but Eve said "no" every time.

"You can't hesitate or they'll follow you for miles!"

"Really? Come on, let me buy you something."

She shook her head. "Buy me lunch later."

We ended up in a mall, nearly a copy of those in Los Angeles. She bought a purse, transferring the contents, and leaving the old one.

Our cell phones worked again, and Eve talked on hers briefly. The frown on her face afterward revived my sense of dread.

"Trouble?"

"No, Felix called Kris, a friend of mine. Wants me to return to work. Can you believe it?" We walked outside the mall.

"Not really. Are you going to call him?"

"Should I?"

"No, stay away from him."

"I guess I should."

"It's up to you. Where's this other place? The other restaurant?"

She giggled: "Not too far," then pointed across a plaza to stairs leading to an outdoor eating area.

"Didn't you say you weren't going near it?"

"I don't care anymore. What can they do?"

I looked up at the place, at a waitress serving tables. Was she a hooker?

There were two messages on my phone. At sea somehow there'd been no service, yet messages got recorded. A reminder of a teeth cleaning appointment and a request from a "Terrence" to reach him as soon as possible regarding "information" I could use. Didn't have a clue what that meant.

Eve took photos of pelicans in some sort of canal, and three kids begged money, which we gave them. The bars looked inviting, but again Eve said "no."

We tired of strolling and went into, of all places, an American-style hamburger shop. I called Terrence -- no answer. Left a message.

"Know anyone named Terrence?" That did it. I saw my concern in her eyes.

"He called you?"

"Yes. Who is he?" When she was silent I asked: "A drug-dealing friend of your husband's?"

"No. He lives next door to Hank -- my brother. They used to work together. I bet he saw that note, and got your number. And overheard you talking. Let's go."

When we hit the street, again, it happened. Fast as a moving roller coaster. Two SUVs, four men, three pistols, open doors, instructions to climb in or die. I'd always said I'd refuse to get into a car at gunpoint. I mean, why bother if a maniac was likely to kill you later? But we got in. Eve cried a tiny bit. I asked them: "What's this about?!" but received no answer. We sped away recklessly.

Guns don't feel good in your ribs, cold blank faces cause your breathing to increase, and racing SUVs accelerate your pulse. Oh how I wanted to repeat my question, to demand an immediate answer. But the gun's nose felt painfully hard, and Eve had one in her ribs from the other side. So we sat quietly, moving from side to side. Nothing I could do. Had it been only me, I'd lunge for the steering wheel up front, get shot, and crash the vehicle. Why not? But Eve was there, so I didn't.

One of the men, Eve's gunman, told the driver, in Spanish, to turn, obviously, because we suddenly swerved up a winding narrow road, and stopped at the top, next to a single-story house. Out we went. Eve was still sniffling. A door opened, a bald young man looked us over, indicated we were to enter, and stepped back. James Bond would have taken the opportunity to kick all their butts. However, I complied. The second SUV, behind us, remained running with the driver in it. The five of us entered, the bald young man closed and bolted the door, and I asked again: "What's this all about?"

"Sit down," was the answer. We did, on a ratty couch. The rest of the room was sparsely, cheaply furnished. A radio was on. The young man pushed the others away, speaking to them in Spanish, and their guns were re-holstered. But now he held one.

"You O'Hara?"

"Yeah. Who are you?"

He grinned. Of course a front tooth was missing. Perhaps I'd be able to knock out the other one.

"Either of you need to go to the bathroom?" When I laughed, the young man laughed, himself. "It's a serious question. Do you?"

"Not me," I said, and looked at Eve, who didn't say a word. "Probably not," I offered. Then it came to me: "Done this before, huh?" I asked the tooth-missing young man.

His kick appeared so graceful, I was surprised to come to on the floor, Eve's kind face leaning over me. The radio was off. A pain swam from my head to my neck and to my head again. "I'm okay," I told her, lying.

Her brother Hank showed up with bottled water, beer, a bag of tacos and harsh words for our captors. He also told Eve she was "safe," as long as she kept her mouth shut. About what, he didn't say, yet it appeared she understood.

I ate a taco and felt the throbbing from the bump on my temple diminish in intensity. "Got any aspirin?" I asked.

He said he hadn't. My assailant smirked. Oh how I wanted to threaten him, or something. But discretion is the better part of valor, as Dad used to say. Eve refused food, but drank water. The other three men had retired to another part of the house, and I asked to use the bathroom. Hank led me to it, stood outside the door, and led me to the couch after he checked my wound. "Sore?"

I smiled. The bald young man paced around, impatient and possibly nervous. Hank drank a beer.

"Anytime you'd care to explain this, that would be fine with me," I said.

"Your mistake was coming on this trip, buster."

"Patrick."

"Right."

"I'm waiting."

Eve put her hand on my arm. "Please," she whispered. "Be nice."

"Great. You know what's going on, they know what's going on, I'm too insignificant to tell. Be nice? I'll be nice. After I say one thing." I looked at my assailant. "You're a punk. How's about you try kicking me without a gun in your hand?" He stepped forward.

"Skip it!" Hank yelled at him. The man turned away. Eve grabbed my arm again, squeezing it. Sure, I understood. We were in danger. She was in danger. Her brother might be a hitman, for all I knew, and this was his gang of back-up murderers.

"I'm nice, I'm being nice," I said, just as my cell phone rang. Hank snapped at the young man: "Idiot! You didn't search him?" He grabbed my phone from my jacket pocket.

"Answer it," I said, inspired. "Might be Terrence."

Bingo. He held the phone, frozen. "What do you know?" he demanded. It stopped ringing. Punk had stepped forward again, more nervous than before.

"Beat it out of me. Just let her go."

Her brother was silent. He carefully put the phone in one jacket pocket, his gun in the other, and stood so close

I could kick him, which naturally, I didn't, considering the situation.

"Look, Peter --"

"Patrick."

"Sure. In approximately one hour you and Eve will be returned to the dock, to take a launch to the ship. Okay?"

"Cool."

"Then you'll go to Los Angeles, okay?" I nodded. "Anything Terrence told you won't matter, then." He checked his watch. "Go," he told Punk, with a jerk of his head. "Leave one man, armed, in a car outside."

Punk eyed me suspiciously, then went to the door. "¡Vamos!" he yelled. That word I knew. The three men came out; they all left without saying anything more. An SUV started up, doors opened and closed. I heard indistinct voices as I suddenly feared for the Hunts. Kidnapping? Worse? Hank took his gun out again, checked outside the door, closed it and came back to us. "He told you what we were doing?"

"Have to beat it out of me, like I said."

"Ha!" he smiled. "Smart ass."

"Let her go, will you?"

"Terrence never talked to him," Eve said, and looked pleadingly at me. "Be nice!"

I laughed. "I am."

Whatever was in the cards for the Hunts, if indeed they were the target, was beyond my control. But, if they didn't show up on the 'Jinx,' would the crew return to Los Angeles? Hank appeared to think so.

"My turn now," Eve said, running to the bathroom as though there wasn't a gun pointed at us. He let her. Good, she didn't fear him. Was he really her brother? I rubbed my head, wanting to warn the Hunts, some way or another, but we were trapped.

Her brother watched me as if I were an animal in a zoo. Then I realized Eve had her phone, too. Although I guessed she wouldn't try using it. She knew what I didn't, like probably it wouldn't help. Who could she call? Just get on the ship, pal, and get away. If he actually meant to let us. Funny, though, I believed him.

Sure enough, in less than an hour, Hank took us outside to the other SUV. It was still daylight, and we all got in, and drove off.

He spoke in Spanish to the driver. Apparently Eve and I were the only people around who didn't know the language. Down the narrow road we went, and through the town. Hank seemed totally unconcerned that we could have jumped out. But why would we attempt to escape? He took us to the dock and walked us to the launch.

"You keeping my phone?" How I wished it would ring again.

"Yes." I was sorry I'd asked, because he said: "Hey," to Eve. "Do you have one?"

She nodded curtly and took it from her new purse and handed it over. What a joke this had become. Then he said:

"Charlie has instructions. Good luck."

We climbed aboard with another couple, probably going to their boat. Hank waited the several minutes until the launch departed. Eve put her face against my shoulder. I wasn't going to ask her a thing. It occurred to me I could get the launch to turn around, but I didn't know where the Hunts were supposed to be, anyway.

The crew couldn't have been more subdued. I drank a beer, at last, regretting not knocking Punk's other front tooth out, and finally got some aspirin. Eve went to her room. The 'Jinx' sailed at seven (6 bells).

There was plenty of food in the dining room. A happier looking Eve joined me. By herself.

Bold as ever, I asked our waiter did he happen to know where the Hunts were?

"They decided to stay. We're going to wait in Wilmington for orders."

Sure. But I asked: "Did you speak with them?"

"Me? No, sir. Charlie must have."

"Thanks." He was clearing the table. So nice of him. I wanted to pound Charlie, now. Was he in on it? Getting a share of the ransom? But, if that were true, we were still in danger. And, huh? What was Hank going to do, hide out the rest of his life? Surely he knew I'd report everything to the police.

"They're not going to kill them, are they?" I asked her. Couldn't help myself.

"My brother? What?"

"Kill the Hunts."

"It isn't what you think. Hank is an agent. An intelligence agent. He's protecting them."

I rubbed my temple. "Say what? From me?"

"He didn't trust you! Captain Hunt is being 'elevated,' they call it. Don't ask me what that means, exactly. Hank is supposed to protect him from terrorists, or whatever. I don't know much."

"So I could have been an assassin? Suppose I'd tossed him overboard on the way here?"

"Not until after the 'elevation.' It wouldn't matter. Once he's moved up the protection is greater. Even I was questionable, because I brought you along. Don't you really get it? Who do you think runs the world? A lot of separate countries?"

"Call me naïve."

"Big business runs the world. You are naïve. Sorry." Now she giggled. "Haven't you ever suspected it?"

"I've suspected a whole lot of things, but --"

"You never heard of the corporatocracy?"

"Yeah, on left-wing, radical media outlets where they also say the moon landings were faked and America is an empire."

"And you don't believe those things?"

1969 -- TRANSITION

Joe knew not to date an actress, but he liked her. When they finished the final play, she drove Joe and Fran and Ron to the city in her parents' car.

He didn't have an apartment anymore, since the payments were too high to keep up during his absence. He'd let it go, figuring to get another in the fall. But summer stock paid so little, Joe found himself in a bad financial position at the end of the run.

Millie offered to put him up, so he moved in with her. They went to the same acting classes, they got along, she had money from home, so why not?

Two bedrooms. His the small one. Millie joked he was her "man," but it didn't feel like that. She'd seen the other actress punch him in the face onstage, when it was supposed to be a swing and a miss. Yeah, right. <u>That</u> actress was a pain. Millie knew it. Everyone knew it. But she sang the *BUS STOP* song like a dream, and delivered her lines in a sexy way the producer-money man liked.

Joe understood why she'd hit him onstage, in spite of her taking up the pretense it was accidental.

Jealousy. Only one night with her and she thought she owned him, bag and baggage. Then all he did was have dinner with Millie on their "dark" night, Monday, and what's-her-name, the singing actress, flipped out. By performance time the following day Joe felt the bad vibe, the "arch" in her voice, and the cold treatment. No problem, he thought. What's-her-name -- Pam, that's it -- would be over it before long and he'd take up where he left off.

That's when they had two weeks to go, one other play, and they'd all be out of there. She got over it, alright. After the torch song Pam had jumped off the table like she always did, strided to Joe's table where he'd been yelling at other customers, on stage, like he was supposed to do, and let it fly. But she connected, her fist clutching the scarf which was part of her get-up. Pow. <u>Supposed to miss</u>.

He had to go on with the play, but his eye swelled up. No knowing how the audience took it.

Sure, she apologized after. She seemed sincere, but she was an actress.

Millie was the one who arrived at the jealousy angle, because Fran told her Pam had mentioned the dinner date, how "fickle" Joe was. Someone had informed Pam about the dinner! No secrets in summer stock, anyway.

So Millie laughed it off, and Pam didn't go to New York like the rest of them. Back to college in Indiana. But Millie and Joe returned to Brocker's Studio to learn more acting.

They'd already done some scenes together, but never gotten romantic. In fact, Millie was the one who'd spotted the notice for the summer venue, on the studio bulletin board, in the spring. So they'd auditioned and got in. $50 a week plus room and board. Six plays starting in July. Eight, really, but Joe was only in six of them.

Now it was September. Joe needed dough. His father had sent him some, earlier in the year -- a thousand -- but that was gone. It might be possible to get more from him but his mean mother didn't want him to be an actor, and it would be very complicated to ask. Fruitless, too, Joe predicted. Sure, he could go home and get into college again. That's what his mean mother wanted. Become a dentist. She just wanted him around. He knew that.

So the summer was over. It was still warm, however, and Joe looked for a part-time job. Millie said not to worry. Her folks sent her lots of money -- five hundred a month for rent, food, and acting class. He could share in it, be her "man."

It started with her calling him in to scrub her back in the bathtub. Which he did. Matter of fact, he loved it -- could see her whole body, could soap up more than just her back. They'd talk about class, and the funny teacher, and plays on Broadway. Millie pretended he wasn't looking at her.

By the third time he did that she leaned her head back with her eyes closed and asked: "What's the matter, don't you want to kiss me? You did it in Maystown."

He had kissed her in Maystown, after Pam's onstage punch, two days after, when he and Millie were in the dressing room. Good kiss, too. Then, also, by the lake on Friday, after lunch. And a couple of times over the weekend. But Joe hadn't pressed onward because she seemed so innocent. Their director, who was older, had asked him what he was waiting for, that last week. Joe was playing opposite Millie in *ANY WEDNESDAY*, a comedy. The director was playing the boyfriend; he could see the sparks flying. But Joe had held off.

Now he washed her underarms, knowing she was waiting for a kiss, her head against the edge of the tub that way.

And Pam was long gone. It had been a tense parting, Pam's last day. She had cried, told him to write, a tad aloof, and walked to the bus. They'd had sex one more time, before that, at the boardinghouse. She'd left Maystown early, not being in *ANY WEDNESDAY*, to go to Indiana, and maybe to New York after graduating from college.

So, he kissed Millie. Warm lips, hot breath, wet arms around his neck, water splashing.

After that Joe slept in the big bedroom. They attended class together, ate meals together, went to Off-Broadway plays together. He did write a letter to Pam. A friendly one. But he didn't mention Millie.

Sometimes they met up with Fran, who was in the Actor's Studio, and Ron, who worked as an usher at the Lincoln Center. That's how Joe got the job. An interview with the fellow in charge, a handshake, and he was wearing a uniform escorting people to their seats. Didn't pay much, but it did wonders for his guilt feelings. He could pay for class at Brocker's, and even lunch and dinner, now and then.

Millie didn't mind, as long as he scrubbed her back with regularity and satisfied her in bed, which wasn't easy.

She found another ad on the billboard. A film short offering two parts. Matter of fact, it only <u>had</u> two parts. They met the director/photographer. No money, but he promised a copy, afterwards, for both of them.

Millie and Joe were picked up on the weekends by the director and his wife who took them to Long Island to film on the beach, get lunch, and return to the city. Fun. There was a guy named Paul who put up the production money, and a guy named Dave who helped with the camera. They rode in another car.

The director/photographer was so meticulous it took almost five weekends to finish. Paul and Dave fell down a cliff in Montauk Point one day, with the camera. They were unhurt, but Millie laughed as they fell, rolling over and over. That delayed the schedule, too.

The finished product looked good, and even though it was only thirteen minutes long, an out-of-state film festival awarded it Best Independent Film Short.

Nothing came of it. Joe and Millie went to class until that December, when she gave it all up and returned to Denver, as innocent as ever. Joe got an acting job touring with *CAT ON A HOT TIN ROOF* in the South. Millie

didn't cry when they said goodbye, sitting in her parents'
car. She was stoic.

"Remember when we were doing that acacia-blossom scene
for class?" After Millie nodded, Joe continued: "That's
when I fell in love with you."

THAT NIGHT

THE DEER HUNTER won the Academy Award for Best Motion Picture achievement that night. I hadn't seen it, although I'd served in Vietnam. Conceivably that fact, of being there, kept me from seeing it. Nevertheless, I was watching the awards in a hotel room in Phoenix, feeling sick.

I'd begun having stomach pain by the time Best Director was announced. A half-hour later I felt unpleasantly weak and nauseous, so I shut off the television and called a friend in Los Angeles, a wannabe actor who said he'd seen the program also. We exchanged our impressions, but I was getting weaker and sicker. I commented how good "John" had looked (Wayne) but he thought I meant "Jon" (Voight), who won for *COMING HOME*. I got off the phone, needing to vomit, but didn't. I felt drugged, sort of: weary, sleepy.

After crawling (nearly literally) into bed, my head swimming in high surf close to drowning, I reasonably hoped it would all calm down when I drifted off. It did, though the pain in my stomach persisted. A very vague impulse to call the front desk zipped across my mind, but the drug-like weariness overwhelmed me, and I slept.

Later a sensation of falling in a wild water-sport ride-tunnel alarmed me, but it ended without me hitting the pool -- instead I was on a field, exhausted, under a wide lovely blue sky and clean, short vegetation around, the whisper of sweet breezes and... a longing to continue. Unmistakable. So, go, get up and walk.

But walking was more like sailing a calm bay, and soon I perceived a wall of some sort, not stones or brick, but... with an opening. An inviting opening. A few figures -- people? -- stood solemnly beyond the entrance, facing me, waiting for me. One dominated the soundless conversation which ensued. Their "words" hit me like splats of electricity.

"You can't come in now. Go back to where you came form." A gesture similar to a man pointing, but not quite the same, accompanied these zapping "words."

"Don't think so, pal," I found myself zinging back at him. "Too late. I'm dead."

"Not quite," he responded. "You may return. Ought to return."

"Sick. Too sick. Pain, too painful."

"We'll help you. You can make it."

A huge, warm, but distant light glowed behind these figures. It seemed complete peace and harmony, drawing my eyes, which nearly burned looking at it.

"If you don't go back a tragedy will ensue," the 'leader' said, zappingly, forcefully. "To pass by us is acceptable if you are willing to allow the slow destruction of your wife, due to this occurrence."

"Occurrence? What is it?"

He smiled, somehow, and a vision of my hotel room appeared. I was twisted uncomfortably in bed, a darkly clothed man stood beside, arranging a cup, a small glass on the table adjacent, taking my limp hand and pressing my fingers against the glass, returning my hand. <u>Suicide</u>, came the startling thought to my mind.

"They're faking your suicide, that's right," one of them confirmed. "She will believe it, will <u>never recover</u>." The zapping was so intense, then, I fell to my knees.

"Never?"

"Never recover, slip into unhappiness, never accomplish her assignment."

"Never recover," the leader repeated.

As soon as I began to agree in my mind to return to the room, I felt the pain in my stomach.

"They poisoned you. And mixed in a chemical to assuage the pain, in your food."

I remembered. The small dinner I'd had <u>had</u> tasted funny, but I'd eaten it anyway.

"Okay," I relinquished. "But I don't like it."

"Of course you don't. But you will be glad you returned, after you rid your body of the poison. Which, unfortunately, will take many years."

"Why so long?"

"It's the way it works. We don't have anything to do with it. Your plan is planned."

"Huh?"

"Your plan, that is, if you return. A long difficult span of years wherein most goods and talent you possessed will be lost. But not lost forever. You'll see."

"Okay," I repeated, not realizing how many years of suffering, how much loss, I was to experience.

"You'll be glad when it's all over," he repeated. "Turn around."

I did. I was swept by another energy (theirs?) from the green field and the wall and the gigantic light, to the tunnel, up through it, and to my bed, my twisted body, asleep.

The morning was a slow one. I didn't feel like going out. I was late to work. They must have thought I had a hangover, which wasn't true. I explained I didn't feel well, but no one appeared to care much. I forced myself to get through the day, dazed, tired, sick to my stomach. The nurse on the film set provided me with Alka-Seltzer, a minor comfort.

I made it through that day, and the next. The hotel doctor took a blood sample, couldn't find anything. Acting was never so hard. I finished the movie in three weeks, weeks of suffering and arguing with the director and the producer who thought I was faking it. Why? Probably due to the negative blood work. I kept my mouth shut, except to say I was sick and that I didn't know why. Skepticism abounded. My wife, from Los Angeles, recommended another doctor. He found nothing, but did say there was "something" in my system, so why not take steambaths? I did, at the hotel, and suffered even more, most likely from detoxing.

The memory of the encounter flitted around like a shy bird, never quite landing. Eventually I dismissed it, but did ask my own doctor to test me for poison.

"Who would have poisoned you?" he scoffingly questioned me. I wanted to say: who gives a shit, just give me the tests!... but I didn't.

My response was simple: "I don't know who would have done it."

His nurse cut my hair and fingernails and I waited several days. Of course the results showed arsenic, and my doctor now had an entirely different attitude.

"You're just below the danger level. I think you're safe. Let's allow the rest of it to come out by attrition."

Attrition? Was that the proper term? He informed me a treatment (B.A.L.) would be advised if I was still in "danger" (which I guessed meant my life), but ramifications in regard to potential organ damage (from the B.A.L. treatment, whatever the hell that was) disinclined him toward using it.

The movie turned out alright, but the director hated me and I was so slow and weak after that, my next few movie roles seemed uninspired, and offers dwindled, and my salary dwindled, and my friends began to shun me, and my reputation was ruined -- "drug use" rumors sprang up seemingly from nowhere. But of course people <u>would</u> assume that, wouldn't they?

My wife and one old friend stuck by me. Love, I guess.

A chiropractor/nutritionist provided me with homeopathic medicine to clean out the arsenic (a heavy metal not easily dislodged from wherever it'd ended up in my system). I exercised, I sweated, I felt pain. Months turned into years.

The memory of the encounter with those doormen (angels?) afforded some comfort, in a bittersweet way: it would eventually be over and I would be "glad." How? When?

One good role did come along. I played a mean person, so it was easier. I felt bad anyway -- that worked in with the performance.

Naturally I wondered who had put poison in my food, food that was in the refrigerator in my hotel room. Someone had gained access to it. How? No one except my wife and one friend believed me, but my idea was, the book. The book which I'd helped the authors research, the book with my name and photo in it, the book which I'd been told by one of the authors never would have been completed without my financial support during its creation, the book which was published a few months prior to the "incident," the book which pointed accusations at government and police high-ups. That explained it, as far as I was concerned.

Of course, the lab report, oddly, didn't help my career, no matter who I showed it to. That was a mystery. Agents frowned at it, questioned me, and handed it back. An Oscar-winning producer expressed curiosity -- but didn't hire me. Most likely the rumors had had a powerful effect. Too powerful. It was like the "Twilight Zone."

But my brave wife went on to produce television shows, and win awards -- shows that gave a positive spin on life, made people feel good, encouraged many to strive for their goals. It was in her character. It must be her "assignment," as they'd told me.

That night was more than 27 years ago. Here I sit, without a job, feeling better physically, waiting, hoping, praying, seeking no answers anymore, only that moment I was told would arrive, when I would be "glad."

TRADITION

Take the risk, Sylvia told herself. Don't be like many women who retreat defensively at the stated predilection for bachelorhood. Find a positive spin, proceed in the face of rejection. Curtis likes single life. So what?

He'd just now said it. He placed his cigarette in the ashtray, looked at Sylvia with those disarming eyes, and smiled:

"My life is fun. What would I want to get married for?"

If she'd hoped to snag him, that hope was lost. Lost! She "swallowed her heart," as they say, and glanced away. Don't fight it. Risk everything. Don't ask rhetorically: "Who said I wanted to marry you?" A coward's route. A trail to tears and excessive drinking and bar-hopping and hollowness. No, agree with him, find common ground.

"I presume that information is meant to drive me away, Curtis, yet it won't. I see that you are sincere. God bless you."

"I'm sorry."

"No need to apologize. My mistake. I inferred incorrectly. Being a bachelor is your choice. Free choice, right? No strings. I had presumed, based on recent behavior, that we might give it a try. In fact, it's obvious you felt a subtle pressure in that direction, or you'd not have said this. Am I correct?"

"No, no, Sylvia. You haven't... well, a little. We have spoken of it. But can't I just love you, and leave it at that?"

Push on: "If it's your natural inclination."

"Well, now, who knows as to natural inclination? I know marriage can ruin a good relationship. Women change, after marriage."

"Is that supported by clinical research?" She refused to laugh. Laughing would be another escape route.

Curtis picked up his cigarette and took a drag on it. He smiled again, quickly, and exhaled. "Personal research. Also"-- he replaced the cigarette in the ashtray -- "men don't want their women to change. Women, in the alternative, want to change their men."

"I've heard that." She drank the dregs of her coffee, wishing it was vodka.

"Sure. After the honeymoon, the clever effort to transform a previously happy man into a well-dressed ass-kissing overachiever begins. That's common knowledge."

Resisting an impulse to kick Curtis under the table, Sylvia sighed, instead, put a hand to her throat, and retorted: "Guys always say that, but what's the harm in dressing right and getting along on the job?"

"No harm. But there's more to it. A woman seeks complete transformation, while the man doesn't. And the woman changes, as I said, contrary to the man's wishes. We want you to remain the way you were."

She took her hand from her throat, and laughed. Curtis continued: "You know. The way you were when we fell in love with you."

"Suppose I'll get fat and sleep all day?" Easy, Sylvia. But her cool was slipping.

"Well, a form of that. You can't help it."

She did kick him. He yelped, and Sylvia stood: "Goodbye, Curtis. Have a nice life."

"Wait!" He jumped up, reaching for her, but Sylvia had moved too fast for him.

She headed for the restaurant door, purse in hand. The world outside waited for her. Curtis followed, yelling: "Stop!" She found the hotel lobby, the entrance, the outside. It was snowing. Curtis was at her side in an instant. A cab driver, standing by his car, looked expectantly.

Easy, girl. See what b.s. he comes up with now. Hope for the best.

"Honey, honey. Where are you going? Why did you kick me?"

"Why? I don't care to be accused of sloth, that's why."

"Sorry. I'm so sorry. It came out all wrong. Let's go inside."

"Curtis, if you love me you'll let me go. You'll find another non-marrying relationship. Don't touch me!" He had tried to put his arms around her. The snow fell softly. The cab driver waited beside his car. A red BMW pulled up in front of Sylvia and Curtis, two men got out, glanced at them, and entered the lobby. The bellman's greeting was cut short by the closing doors.

This isn't so bad, she thought. He can't let me go. But it _is_ cold. Be strong, be calm.

"I don't care to let you go. Come inside, we'll thrash this over, you'll tell me your preferences, I'll tell you mine."

"Yours are crystal clear. And mine are patently obvious. I can't go on dating you without an end in sight."

"Please. What 'end'? We've been happy."

"Happiness can't -- we aren't going to make it <u>your way</u>. It isn't enough for me." There: put up or shut up. Propose or f--- off.

"Sylvia." She permitted him to place one arm around her, and pull her under the overhang, out of the gentle snowfall. "Do you want to marry me? Are you serious?"

She looked up at him, wondering what to reply. Say yes and he'll explain his single's philosophy again, say no and he'll have won. She said nothing.

"Can't I just love you? Don't you see? I love you."

"And I love you." That might work. It was true, but did he care? Was it as important to him as to her? Curtis slowly smiled. The cab driver got back into his car, waiting. Sylvia waited. Now or never.

Curtis responded weakly: "See, we love each other. Can't we continue like this?"

"No." She pushed him off. He looked stricken. "Until you are willing to commit, I'll never trust you fully." There, she said it. Good girl. "What's acceptable in a relationship from your point of view is not, from mine." Said it doubly.

"Honey, I know." An elderly woman exited the lobby, the electric doors startling Sylvia. The woman was wearing an expensive full-length coat, and a fur hat. The cab driver got out of his car. Curtis stared at the falling snow. Sylvia waited, even though the cold had chilled her so extensively she began to shake. Her risk-taking resolve was nearly gone -- he had about thirty seconds left.

"But"-- he protested. "Can't we --"

"No, we can't, I've told you. Better decide one way or the other, here and now."

Curtis' disarming eyes caught her fierce ones. "If we do get married, may I stay the way I am?"

"Of course."

MAINLY BECAUSE

Today Tom twisted that last piece of bothersome logic
(which had taken residence in the back of his mind,
opposing one of his chief aims in life: honesty) into a
formless hunk of nothing, and figuratively tossed that
piece of logic into a figurative trashcan. Tom's heart won
out against his intellect, reducing that long-held
rationale: "It's not gentlemanly to hurt another's
feelings, even with truth," to dust.

Today Tom forged ahead, fearfully abandoning logic,
turning toward the unknown, timidly, spurred by the loud,
incessant 'call' of his goal, of honesty, and sent a letter
to Jack. Jack, his ex-friend, Jack the miser, Jack the
tormentor who had <u>effortlessly</u> refused to loan Tom money
when it was so needful, Jack who held money in estimation
higher than long-lasting friendship.

The mailing done, the overcast sky darkening, the
after-work traffic thickening, the decision made, the act
fulfilled, Tom toasted his difficult decision with shots of
golden brown whiskey while Charles Bronson played his
banged-up harmonica in *ONCE UPON A TIME IN THE WEST* via
Tom's DVD player.

Sad, but satisfied, he watched the classic story unfold, grimly noting the <u>love of money</u> displayed by Henry Fonda's character, and others, to the sound of haunting music and sudden gunfire. The contents of the letter intruded upon his evening, coming to mind perhaps a half-dozen times, but by the end of the movie Tom was warmly feeling how good it was to be alive, and how lucky Jason Robards had been to slap Claudia Cardinale on the behind. Jack would know the letter's truth, the mistake he'd made withholding a simple loan, of losing a close friendship because of, mainly because of, that. His letter pointed out the statistical shallowness of Jack's refusal: less than one-tenth of his modest fortune was asked for, an insignificant amount to sacrifice to assist a long-time friend in need.

By morning the decision against logic felt increasingly just, the past reluctance gone forever. A new day, an escape from the one before, a spring forward unshackled by fear. Fear of hurting Jack, who deserved, now, nothing, nothing save Tom's clarifying message, clarifying what Jack should have known anyway. Putting the complaint into words lifted the pain from his heart, and if it added a fraction to Jack's heart, so be it. Jack's wife had never liked him, of that he was convinced; she would be glad the friendship had ceased. She would welcome this turn of events, welcome a future void of Tom, void of pretending she enjoyed his company. She could cling to Jack forever -- what did he care? She'd enjoy the freedom -- no more visits, no more phone calls, no more wondering when her husband would return from lunches, from long conversations the friendship had elicited over those many years.

Tom was free too, although he'd gained much from conversations with Jack (a blessing, however, which had dwindled when Tom's fortune had dwindled). The insightful advice Jack provided re Tom's many, various romances had always helped, but that was over. What problems Tom may have, now, with women, he'd have to handle himself. So be it.

That next day his work was the same, no better or worse, as a result of mailing the letter of explanation -- but Tom was more cheerful. Sweeping and mopping was the same has always, but less tiring now the goal was accomplished, the burden lifted, the message mailed. Yes, Jack's advice had dwindled, patience had dwindled, interest showed re Tom's romances had dwindled. The less money Tom made, the less time Jack could find for him. A stunning realization which oddly only had come to Tom in the end, though the evidence of Jack's growing impatience, lessening of interest, withholding of guidance had been apparent for years. Tom had never guessed the reason, merely noticed the trend painfully, hoping all along it would reverse. Now he knew: it was mainly because of money.

WHAT'S WRONG WITH THIS PICTURE?

Arecely and I had continued as girlfriend and boyfriend, that year, following the shooting. I had killed the creep who was attacking her. It all came out -- tons of publicity, news photos, TV interviews.

Her parents didn't care for the notoriety, and even Arecely gradually grew weary of it all. For some strange reason I liked it. Probably because I was the hero. Anyway, we went on with part-time law school and our loving relationship, the dead man nearly forgotten in six months or so. Not quite, of course. And one of my classes touched on the permissible use of deadly force -- which my conduct threw into question. But the law is clear -- it's okay because I'd reasonably believed my life was in immediate danger.

Now, oddly enough, we were driven into another mystery. Whether it was a murder mystery or not remained to be seen. Officer Figari of homicide had jokingly ordered us not to become embroiled in any more police business -- and we'd agreed. But as I always say: "Whatever happens is what happens."

Arecely didn't want to move in together, so we didn't. In fact, she'd stayed with her sister a while to recover from the incident. I cut down on my smoking; she cut down on using the f-word. Her parents sent her money for school, and I continued working as a vendor. She was ahead of me, class-wise, and the gap extended because I wasn't able to take a full part-time load. Too busy traveling around.

My uncle's neighbor's wife was found drowned in their pool -- the neighbor claiming shock and dismay and 'lack of knowledge' of the circumstances. How she died was no mystery -- lungs full of pool water. <u>Why</u> she died an inquest attributed to her bumping her head, accidentally, on the edge of the pool, losing consciousness, and drowning. My uncle thought not. He told the investigators he'd overheard angry fights, for weeks, next door. The police couldn't prove the husband's involvement, accepting his story of being asleep at the time -- the pool was a long distance from the house. He appeared genuine, on TV news coverage, expressing sorrow and pain at the death of his wife.

Arecely, too, felt he looked sincere. Only Sam, my uncle, doubted it: "Liar," he called him. "Out-and-out liar."

The only thing that troubled me was the 'accidental' head injury. Unlikely. It was her swimming pool, after all. But she'd been drinking -- that was proved. And the husband had no record other than one DUI years earlier. No assault charges, no reports of domestic violence. Still... Sam had heard loud fights on many occasions.

Arecely and I did have a class together -- Evidence, Part One. Luckily we could study with each other -- it was a tough one. Especially the 'character evidence' part. So complicated. When is evidence of character admissible in court, when is it not?

Like I said, a year had gone by, and we took the finals. Summer break. Not long, though, because we were supposed to take a class during the summer (except I was granted permission to skip it due to my work schedule). Arecely signed up for Administrative Law.

During the break we'd visited her folks in San Antonio, a beautiful city. They liked me okay, but it was uncomfortable -- she and I stayed in one bedroom. But nobody mentioned it. Cool people. Her mother had been born in Honduras. I tried out my Spanish, to little avail.

We were both happy when the plane returned us to Burbank Airport. She reminded me it was where we'd first met: on an airplane, awaiting deplaning, when she'd told me she was psychic. Not exactly a joke, as events later showed.

We drove to my apartment after getting our luggage, and food from Del Taco.

"Hotshot," she called me, as usual, "I'm going to sleep. I'm very tired."

"Sure. Go ahead."

"Don't wake me up with that 'Can I rub oil on you?' trick."

"I haven't done that in months."

"That's what I mean. You're thinking about it again."

"Just how do you know that?"

"I'm --"

"Psychic. I remember."

She kissed me and went to the kitchen and went to the bathroom and went to bed. I stood on the balcony having a cigarette. She didn't like me to smoke inside when she was there. I thought about the woman in the pool, the bad bump on her head, the husband's expressions of dismay. I wanted to ask Arecely if maybe he'd overdone it, in her opinion, but decided to wait until the morning.

In the morning, I didn't feel like asking her because, with light in the sky and coffee in my stomach, I didn't care so desperately, figuring she'd scoff at the idea anyway. Instead I played an Eagles' CD and pondered the ramifications of "The Long Run." Sweet music it is.

There were eight days to go before my next classic car show, in Cincinnati, Ohio, and Arecely had put pressure on me to take her somewhere. But where, exactly? We hadn't the money for another trip.

She went to lunch with two female student friends, and then on to her apartment, where we'd first made love. Funny I often thought of it that way. Arecely had worked again, after the shooting, as a receptionist, but the memories haunted her, so she quit. Her folks understood, took a loan on their property, and funded her studies. I was haunted, too, but both parents being dead and a brother struggling to provide for his family gave me no access to extra cash.

She called me at three:

"Hey, hotshot, what are you doing?"

"Pretending I'm rich."

"Oh, great. Can I have a new car?"

"Depends. How much is it?"

"Don't be a miser. You're rich, aren't you?"

"And want to stay that way."

"Hey, after I pass the bar I'll provide for you, until you do. Relax."

"Okay, I'm relaxed. How was lunch?"

"Fine. We're all complaining about the exams and waiting for our grades, like you."

"Not me. I just want to pass, that's all."

"Listen, Ed, I've been thinking about the Nichols drowning."

"Again?"

"Like you haven't?"

"No comment."

"Right. So... I'm wondering: couldn't he crack her head, hold her underwater, dry his clothes, go to bed, escape detection?"

"Sure. Your point?"

"My point. If the detective questioned him aggressively, he might slip up. Hmmmm?"

I laughed. "Could work. Only I'm not calling Figari to suggest it. You do it."

"Chicken."

"Maybe. He won't like us interfering with another case, he --"

"It's closed! You know, case closed."

"Correct." There was a pregnant pause. She sighed. "Alright, chicken. I'll ask him."

"You'll have to push him. He won't be very much interested, I bet."

"I'll push him."

So, she phoned Figari. Déjà vu all over again. Unfortunately (or was it?) he declined to bring Mr. Nichols in for an interview, 'aggressive' or otherwise. But Arecely reported he'd seemed interested in her theory. Figari had learned his lesson not to doubt her.

"What about surveillance?" I offered.

"Us?"

"No, no. Him! The police!"

"Oh, well, he -- I did ask about that -- he wouldn't even consider it. You know how by-the-book he is. Not like us, right?"

"Stop it. We are not going to follow that guy around on our own. Definitely not."

"Okay, tough guy. Have it your way."

"Please, Arecely. I'd have to take my gun with me, and then he might spot us, and then --"

"I know. It's dangerous."

"Could be, especially if he's guilty."

"Think so?" Another pregnant pause.

"Well," I answered slowly, "it does strike me he overplayed his remorse a bit."

"Me, too. We should talk more often. Are you scared to confide in me?"

"Sort of. But, look, that's not persuasive evidence. We need a confession, or a witness, or someone he told about it."

"That's hearsay, isn't it? Can't use it."

"Next semester's material. But I've been reading ahead. There are exceptions to the hearsay rule, and what they called 'exclusions.' Hearsay isn't always objectionable."

"How so?"

"I haven't read that far. We'll learn it in the fall."

"Can't wait! What if Nichols hits the road, disappears, runs away?"

"Arecely, we can't prevent that. <u>And</u>," I tried to be forceful, which didn't always work with her, if ever -- "there's little chance we can find a person who heard Nichols say anything incriminating. Where would we start looking?"

"He must have a few friends, co-workers, whatever."

"Oh boy."

"Why not, hotshot?"

"Please. Suggest it to Figari."

She hung up on me. Not the first time.

I had a new partner for the vending business. He was young, black, and a hard worker. My old partner, Robert, quit, begging off because of 'burned-out' syndrome. The traveling, the erratic income, the heavy boxes of T-shirts and classic car photos. But the real reason was my shooting the creep. Robert was not capable of dealing with it. But Lionel was the man. Cool, friendly, occasionally funny. Used to work delivering UPS parcels to offices -- doctors, mostly. Guess he got tired of it. Still lived with his folks. Anyway, we met for discussions in preparation of the next several car shows. I arranged for the airplane flights -- the next shows were out of state.

Arecely called me.

"Come on, I'm sorry. Come over." She was always to the point.

"Beg."

"No."

"Okay. Say please."

"Please."

"Okay."

I went to her apartment, bringing take-out, as usual. Her mother's recipes didn't work for me, and except for pasta Arecely couldn't cook anything but them -- who knew why.

We ate, and she talked about her upcoming class. I talked of my upcoming jobs. We avoided, for the most part, any mention of the drowning. Until the after-dinner decaf. Boy, did she mention it. Must have been why she asked me over.

"Figari wasn't mean in the least. He answered every one of my questions politely."

"Shocking."

"It <u>was</u>. I said you had reservations, but <u>I</u> felt the death suspicious."

"Um-hm."

"<u>And</u>"-- she actually smirked -- "he offered to take a look at the crime scene report, the lab reports, the --"

"He called it a 'crime' scene, or you did?"

"He did."

"Interesting."

"Yes, interesting. More decaf?"

"How about real coffee?"

"Umm. You mean 'regular'?"

"Regular." She left the tiny living room and prepared it. I wondered about the 'crime.' The detective may have been humoring her because he felt that last experience had been upsetting to her -- which it had. Plus he liked her. Or he truly felt a double-check of the facts was warranted. When Arecely returned, I conceded:

"If Figari finds problems with the reports, or... significant questions, I'll, you know, get into it with you. But"-- before she could reply, I added: "don't think we'll put ourselves in the middle of it. That Nichols may be dangerous."

"Yep. Maybe. Who's arguing that?"

"I'm only saying --"

"Let me get your coffee." She went rather too fast to the kitchen. I had to admit there was a surge of excitement accompanying my resistance. What if Nichols <u>had</u> killed his wife? Someone needed to find out.

When she returned I recommended we look up the newspaper reports and study them. That got me a kiss.

In Los Angeles you see, occasionally, gorgeous sunsets. That next day I saw one. The west was light blue at the horizon, and very red, slightly above, where the clouds masked the sky. Higher was darker. My mood matched the sunset. I couldn't tell whether the sun was below the horizon, but I guessed it hadn't set, yet, producing the beautiful red clouds. The dark above matched my dread, the bold color, my excitement, the rich blue, my calm fearlessness. Three moods in one.

Arecely had looked up the newspaper articles that day, and we'd pored over them. Nothing spectacularly unusual: most of it we already knew. Except Nichols used to run a private detective firm, many years ago. He'd gone on to another business, Hollywood publicity, public relations, and then retired. His wife had been his partner. She'd been well known and loved by the 'Hollywood elite,' it said, but we guessed the lack of specific star names meant <u>not</u> the elite, but more probably the <u>less</u> than elite.

Of course she may have had an affair with a star, or pseudo star, and Nichols killed her for it. Or, he had an affair, and she reacted badly, and he killed her for that.

I drove to my apartment, to the west, feeling and seeing the red turn to a gentler rose, and parked in the underground. Arecely had tried to find out the name of the public relations, or publicity firm, he'd owned, or ran. No luck. Newspapers didn't give out info like during Raymond Chandler days.

I walked up the short outside steps to my door. No note there curtly warning me off the case, no mysterious package on the mat, no signs of breaking and entering. I hadn't truly expected those things, but I did look for them.

Inside I first drank water, then opened a beer, then remembered to do some sit-ups and push-ups. Never know, Nichols could discover our investigation and a conflict might ensue.

After showering I returned to my beer. Okay, Ed, what's this all about? Couldn't think of a thing. Needed

more info. Oh, yes, call my uncle. What else did he know?
Tomorrow. I had another beer, wondering what Arecely was
thinking.

Sam invited me to lunch at Carrow's in Northridge when
I explained my purpose. He was taller than me, an ex-
Marine, and moderately disabled by a wound to his right arm
sustained in Lebanon, in '83. Sam hadn't been in the
barracks when it was blown up, but was injured rescuing men
from the rubble. And seeing all those dead bodies had made
him distant, emotionally. He'd never been the same.

We sat in the rear of the coffee shop. He ordered
coffee. I had a good roast beef sandwich and lemonade.

"Well, Eddie, what you been up to?"

"Same old stuff. Law classes, selling memorabilia at
car shows. You know."

That satisfied him. I said: "This woman. You knew
her?"

"Sure. Crazy, though. Swam at night. And during the
day. Drank a lot."

"So I understand. Ever talk to her?"

"A time or two. She'd wave from the pool. My rear
fence ain't that high. I talked to her. Him, he was nice

enough. But I didn't like him. Big shot. You know.
Never swam."

"Sure. Did they -- I mean, you said they argued. Did
you hear what about?"

He drank coffee. I waited patiently.

"Couldn't figure it. Some business stuff. Money."

"Not their relationship?"

"No, but well, he didn't like her swimming naked.
That much I heard."

"What?"

"Yeah. Didn't I tell you? She was always naked.
Even during the day."

"You could see her?"

"Yep. Especially from the guest room over my garage."
He laughed.

"Good body?"

He shrugged. "Most are, to me. Not heavy. She got
lots of exercise." He laughed again. "What's your point?"

"That night -- hear anything special?"

He looked suspiciously at me. "She screamed, he
hollered. But... I didn't hear no physical stuff --
physical fighting."

"Did you look over?"

"No! I was in the den. But the windows were up. I didn't want nothin' to do with it, let me tell you."

"Sure. Couldn't you make out their words? It's important. Like I said, maybe they argued about some subject related to the... death."

"The murder? All I heard special was: 'Keep it up, you'll regret it,' like I told the cops. Mrs. Nichols yelled that."

"Um-huh." He seemed nervous. I changed the subject: "Ever speak to Chloe?"

"Yeah. Needs a tooth implant, but she's okay."

From my advanced reading in Evidence, Part Two, about hearsay exceptions and exclusions, I found a significant fact that could be applied to this case. First of all, my uncle had seemed nervous. Did he know more than he was telling? Had he seen or heard anything beyond what he told the police? And me? He might be afraid -- why not? Maybe Nichols would kill him if my uncle implicated him.

Evidence law allows a witness, like my uncle, to relate in court other people's comments -- people who are not in court to testify to them. Like Mrs. Nichols. Of course testifying to another's comments is not normally permitted, as per the hearsay rule. I'd learned, however, a vast array of special circumstances can make the non-permitted, permitted. Like certain death-bed comments overheard by the witness. They're permitted. And so many others I'd jokingly warned Arecely would be on the next exam.

If my uncle had heard Mrs. Nichols yelling, for instance, "Don't do it. Stop! Don't kill me!" and he could swear it was her voice, the rule says he can testify to it. And help convict Nichols.

But how to get Sam to own up? Assurances of police protection? He was smart enough to know that was available, and still be too scared to make a statement. Arecely might convince him to talk -- she could charm just about anyone.

I called her. Oh, she loved my suspicions, but, crazily, begged off:

"Not me. If he's afraid, I wouldn't want the responsibility. You do it."

"You mean... if something happened to him?"

"Exactly."

"But he won't -- I don't think I'd succeed. Even _if_ I took the responsibility."

"You can be pretty persuasive when the occasion requires it."

"I like the sound of that. Should I come over tonight?"

"No," she laughed. "First decide if you want to persuade him to talk. Then get him to. Then come over."

That evening I felt an intense pressure to put pressure on Sam, and a diametric conflict not to introduce him to potential harm. Arecely was right. My only way out was to confer with Det. Figari, who wasn't in when I called. They could protect him. They could make an arrest and keep the culprit in jail. Although possibly a judge would grant bail, Nichols having no record (as I recalled) save a DUI. My tension increased until 9 o'clock when an idea struck me: search Sam's house, look for anything. But that was foolish. What would be there? Notes containing Mrs. Nichols' pleas for help, or a tape recording of Sam recounting what he might have heard? Absurd.

I went to bed early, satisfied a talk with Figari was the way to proceed. Even that, I knew, could place Sam in an awkward spot. Figari may investigate, and Nichols could learn why.

In the morning I felt refreshed. <u>I'd speak to Sam</u>. Hey, he could tell me things in confidence; we would decide what to do about it. I phoned him. Being retired, he answered, said he was free all day. I lied, kind of, expressing a wish to go to the Getty Museum. More or less true -- I <u>did</u> want to go. Just not necessarily that day.

At his house I said I didn't really feel like going to the Getty. "If you don't mind. Let's eat at the Claim Jumper."

"Yeah, why not? You buyin'?"

The coolest waitress in the world worked there. Not that I could pronounce her name. Black hair, trim body, enticing lips. I got my usual half Cobb Salad without bacon, Sam had a humungous hamburger with a name like "Widow Maker." The waitress visited our table often, pouring me decaf and replacing Sam's strawberry lemonade, sweetly laughing at my dumb jokes.

"When you leaving town again?" he asked.

"Thursday," I replied. "Next week."

"Where to?"

"Kansas City."

"Never been there."

"It's a nice town."

"Umm." Sam ate his giant burger.

"Say, I spoke with Arecely about what you told me, about the night Mrs. Nichols drowned, and --" I forced a smile -- "she's funny, she's constantly --" The waitress whose name I couldn't pronounce came by again.

"Anything else? More coffee?"

"No," I replied, looking at her breasts. She caught me, so I quickly added, pointing to her name-tag: "How do you say that again?"

"Zah-feer!" She giggled, and even leaned forward to show me. Did she guess I hadn't been staring at the name-tag? Probably.

"Oh, yeah, Sofrear."

"Zah-feer!"

"I thought it was 'Sophie,' or --"

"A lot of people do when I first say it." So nice of her -- but not likely.

"No more coffee, thanks." She left. I watched her, and then thought of Arecely. Oops.

"Uh... yeah. You know how she is. She thinks maybe you aren't telling all you heard. Could that be true?"

"Man, are you nuts? Why would I hold back on something like that?"

"Because..." I didn't want to say it, but did: "Maybe for fear Nichols will do something." Sam just looked at me. "To protect himself. If he killed her."

"I didn't hear nothin' more than I told you. I said I <u>thought</u> he killed her."

So much for that. I reported to Arecely. She was disappointed in me: not enough pressure on Sam.

"But he won't confide in me if he truly fears that Nichols --"

"I know. Skip it, hotshot. When does he leave his house?

"Huh? Hardly ever."

"Grocery shopping? A date? A movie?"

"Say -- what...? Oh, I get you. I already thought of that. What's the good?"

"Don't know. It's my instinct. Psychic, remember?"

"I'll search, okay, but by myself."

"Fine. Don't get caught."

"Sam wouldn't hurt me."

"No, surely not. But can you get in?"

"Easy. He gave me a key years ago."

"You lie."

"I am not lying. Can I come over?"

"After you find something interesting."

I didn't find anything interesting, but I went to Arecely's for the night, two nights later, anyway. Sam's place was more neatly kept than I'd expected. Maybe he had a part-time housekeeper, like me, although he'd never mentioned it. I did find a lot of old magazines, most with naked women in them. No wonder his wife left him. She must have found his hiding place. And there was a box of photos in his bedroom closet, photos of women on the beach and at the park. But no diary, no notes, no tape recordings. And no way I was going into his computer, even though Arecely urged me to.

She woke me up, in bed, with an idea. Not the idea I expected.

"Did you find his camera?"

"Yes."

"Well, maybe he has pictures in it we'd want to see."

"Please! Like Nichols drowning his wife?"

"Why not?"

I had no good answer for that, so we concocted a story: she'd break-and-enter this time while I went with him to the mall to buy her a birthday present. Not that it was really her birthday. He fell for it, easily believing I needed help. He knew me.

And once again the two of us, law students, conspired to, _and_ broke, the law. Figari wouldn't like it. Our professors wouldn't like it. I didn't like it. Only Arecely liked it, and stole his film out of his camera. Burglary.

The next day I left for Kansas City. She'd have the pictures, such as they were, developed, and 'let me know.' Great. She liked the present, too. From Victoria's Secret.

My flight departed from Burbank Airport, with a connection in Denver, and on to K.C. A young girl at the gate in Burbank caught my attention -- as occasionally they do. She yawned, she glanced at me twice, she spoke with a man nearby. She was too far away for me to hear their conversation, which was just as well. I'd likely be irritated if the man said something fascinating and aroused her interest. Her light brown hair was fairly short, her blouse hidden by a jacket, her legs covered by jeans. During the boarding process fate placed her directly in front of me, and as we climbed the steep ladder to the commuter airplane I could have, but didn't, look closely at her rear end. Didn't seem fair to take advantage of the moment, or fair to Arecely at <u>all</u>.

I noticed, nevertheless, she wore a small backpack which read: *UCLA Bruins*, so I surmised she was a student there. I wanted to ask her what she was studying, but that would require a few preliminary remarks, which I wasn't able to formulate. Fate was good, again, and placed her in the row across the aisle from me. I was in an aisle seat and so was she. But prior to takeoff the young girl, who I decided must have <u>gone</u> to UCLA and now was graduated, because she wasn't <u>that</u> young, moved over to the empty window seat in her row. Probably watching the world outside was more interesting than watching me. Funny, though, the man in my row made an odd remark when the flight attendant asked us if we wished to move forward, since the flight was far from full, with other seats available. We were in the last row, and apparently the attendant assumed we'd want to escape its confines. I told her: "No, thanks," as did my companion, and the young

girl. I added: "I don't mind sitting here."

The man next to me said: "This is where the important

people sit, like a limousine." I guessed it was a joke,

but it afforded me the opportunity to turn to the young

girl and ask:

"Do you agree? Is this where the important people

sit?" I remembered to laugh, always a good thing to do

when I made a joke. Which that was, kind of. She

pleasantly responded in the affirmative, and her brief

laugh relieved my tension -- she knew it was a humorous

aside.

Later I made another comment to her, and she to me,

but the aisle and empty seat between us made conversation

difficult. Plus by then I'd spotted what appeared to be an

engagement ring on her finger -- or worse, a fancy wedding

ring. Oh how I wanted to say: "You're too young to get

married. Why not live a little?" But naturally I didn't.

And I wanted to ask if she was going to UCLA and tell her I

was a student myself, even though fast approaching fifty.

Didn't say that either.

In Denver fate placed her beside me at the flight

monitors. I spoke again: "Looking for your gate number?

I couldn't hear the announcement either." She responded "Yes!" And "Gate 23," as she spotted it on the board.

"I'm right next to you," I said, "24." She smiled sweetly and we walked together a bit. I thought of Arecely and said: "See you," and turned into a newsstand, for no good reason.

"'Bye," my maybe still a student, maybe not, maybe engaged, maybe married fellow passenger said, and I felt awful: would I ever see her again? I liked her manner, I liked her looks, I liked her easy-going friendliness and undercurrent of intelligence. But... I already had a girlfriend in her twenties. What was I thinking? Are all men like me? Women think so, of course.

My gate was not next to hers: the display showed '27'. In fact, I'd heard the announcement on board, which I thought was '24' but sort of lied telling her I hadn't. Have to quit that -- 'sort of lying.' It's nearly the same as 'truly' lying, isn't it?

This girl was intriguing to me beyond the normal 'passerby' encounter. Why, I wondered? Her look: a touch of party-girl, a few too many parties and drinks, a smartness, a kindness. But, the ring. And she wasn't cold like many girls from the Los Angeles area. So, I braved a

last word with her, going to gate 23's seating area. I saw
her, I stopped, I waved. She saw me, she smiled
beautifully, waved back.

"Nice talking to you. Have a good life," I yelled,
stupidly, yet meaning it.

"You too," she yelled back, seemingly meaning it.

"I'm Ed," I yelled. And that great smile appeared.

"Tracie," she responded, probably not aware of how
kind it was of her to offer it.

Kansas City with tall buildings, many steakhouses --
an old cattle town -- and talkative cab drivers. I had
worked here before -- two years or so ago. Time flies,
most definitely. The hotel room was small but adequate,
the bed firm, the towels clean. What more did I need? I
called Arecely. No answer. Left a brief message. I
thought of Tracie, hoping she did have a good life.

I thought of Mrs. Nichols. She wouldn't have one,
now. Who killed her? No one? An accidental drowning? I
watched the news and fell asleep.

After coffee, exercise, and a shower, in the morning,
I called Lionel's room. He'd flown in later. No answer.
I ate in the downstairs café and took a cab to the

Convention Center. Many exhibitors were still setting up their vending booths, sharp cars were everywhere; I searched around, looking for my stand, and my partner, wondering if I should call Arecely again.

Simultaneously my phone rang -- her -- and I saw Lionel at our booth, laying photos out on two tables.

"Hello?"

"Hey, hotshot. Up yet?"

"Sure I'm up. I'm already at the show."

"Really?"

"There's a two-hour time difference, remember?"

"Oh, yeah. But... they haven't opened the doors yet, have they?"

"No, it opens late on Friday."

"Uh-huh. Well, I took a look at the pictures."

"And?" I had reached our stand by then, waved, shook Lionel's hand, and walked off again. He saw I was on my cell phone.

"Sam has shots of her in the pool, nude."

"You're kidding."

"And pictures of other people I don't know, in a backyard."

"None of him?"

"One." She made me wait. Just like her.

"And?"

"He's standing by the pool. She's in the water."

"Wow."

"<u>Yes</u>. But who took it?"

"Could be remote, or time-delayed."

"I think it was. He used a long lens. I saw it with the camera."

"Me too. Does this mean he got mixed up in it? Nichols caught him there?"

"Don't know. You have to ask him."

"Right. Fun. He lied to me."

"<u>And</u> to the police."

We sold some pictures and posters until 9 pm. I'd talked to Arecely again. She wanted to tell Figari. I said no, we'd swiped the film. <u>She'd</u> swiped the film. We were in a tough spot. Could I get away, leave the show, return to L.A. to confront Sam? I asked Lionel about it, telling him he could keep all the money we made Saturday and Sunday. He readily agreed. Of course I had to 'sort of' lie about my reasons.

The following morning I checked out of the hotel, returned to the airport and to Burbank. Arecely met me at my place to swap ideas.

"Let's say Nichols caught them in the pool," I offered.

"*In* the pool?"

"Why not?"

"He's dressed. Look."

I'd examined the photos already. "Well, sure. Ever heard of a man undressing?"

"True," she answered. "He may have."

"And jumped in. Maybe it was their regular practice."

"Sam? Such a stupid move, if they were caught..."

"Men do stupid things."

"True."

"And after he left, Nichols came out, banged her head, and pushed her under the water."

"Sick."

"And Sam knew, or guessed it, and lied, of course, later."

Arecely was drinking water, me, beer. She drank and nodded her head. "Eddie -- do you really want to pursue this? He's your uncle."

"I don't want to pursue it. But if she was murdered, her husband can't go free. He might do it again, someday, to someone else." Now I drank. She had a gentle look in her eyes:

"Not to mention... you know, we can't avoid this... Sam could have done it. Honey?"

I'd thought of that on the airplane. "What was his motive?"

"You'll have to ask him." When I didn't respond she added: "It's only a theory."

We decided a question or two of Det. Figari might help. I had to be careful, however, not to mention the photo. But reaching him was difficult -- always on a case, it seemed, out in the field. By Tuesday he returned my call.

"Hello, Eddie. How are you?"

"Fine, fine. You?"

"Can't complain. Busy. Still seeing Arecely?"

"Yes. Still seeing her. Do you have anything new on the Nichols drowning?"

"No. It's not my case, is it?" Sarcasm.

"Should be. Head bashed against the edge of the pool, supposedly no witnesses."

"Yeah, well... there some new evidence?"

Rather than lie I pushed on: "Was the body overly traumatized? Too much force used?"

"Not according to the pathology report. I did look for that, believe it or not."

"Right. Of course. One more thing. Did Nichols get any big money, like from an insurance policy?"

Figari laughed. "I checked that too. He hasn't got it, yet, but it wasn't large. Fifty thousand, maybe.

"That's huge."

"Listen, Ed. That's nothing compared to the estate his wife left him. It was all hers, not community property. Close to two million. He inherits it, though, from her will."

"Yikes. Motive, man! Are you saying he wasn't rich himself?"

"No, it doesn't appear that way. She had the money. He was retired, but --"

"Okay, you're on to something. How can we prove it?"

"Prove he killed her? Don't know. We need more evidence. If he killed her. I tend to agree with you here. But there's nothing else as far as I can see. To go on."

"But... how about questioning my uncle again? You know, he could have heard more than he said. Might have seen something weird and, and, he's afraid to talk."

"Is that your impression?"

"It is, I hate to say it."

"Is he the kind who'd scare easy?"

"Easy? Anyone would be scared."

"Or Nichols bought his silence?"

"That's... quite possible. Sam is acting strange, I'll tell you. Nervous about it."

"Alright. I'll... this Arecely's idea?"

"Pretty much."

"Figures. I'll have a talk with him."

I bought a newspaper at the stand near my apartment, said hello to Lefty, who now ran the place, drove through Del Taco for lunch and arrived at my front door believing, now, that Nichols killed her for the almost two million. Still we needed to find out what more Sam knew. Had he been joining her in the pool, or was that photo a one-time deal? Was he obsessed with her? I knew the top of the stairs over his garage looked down on that pool -- not blocked by trees. He may have watched her out the guest room window. He'd lived alone since the divorce. Lonely? Did he have other pictures of her? Or her with Nichols?

I ate my burrito and called Aracely to tell her what Figiai had said. She wasn't surprised at it, and was pleased he planned on questioning Sam further. I took a nap. Lionel then left a message which I played when I woke up. He was back from the show. I called Arecely:

"Hey, honey," I said. "What's up?"

"Nothing. Just took a shower."

"Nice and clean now? Dried off yet?"

"Stop it. Hear from the detective?"

"Not yet! Give him a day or two."

"I'm impatient. You know me."

"I know you. Who do you think those other people are? In Sam's pictures?"

"Looked like a... a party in someone's backyard. He's your uncle. If you don't recognize them, how would I?"

"Only asking. It's not his yard, I can tell you that."

"You already did."

"Right. Guess it doesn't matter."

"Might. No stone unturned is my motto."

"And the shot of him -- there's no towel, no swimsuit."

"We already discussed this. He could have undressed. No suit required. What's odd about the photo?"

"Something is, huh?"

"I think so. Look at it."

I picked it up. "I am."

"See something funny?"

"No. Wait. She's not looking at him."

"Right. Where's she looking?"

"Past him, I think. She's not happy, either."

"So Nichols came out right at that moment."

"Perhaps. And they fought. But my uncle's tough, an ex-Marine. He'd have won."

"She'd run into the house."

"Sam would follow her."

"They'd have sex."

"Come on, now. You don't think that."

"Sure I do. Good sex."

"And Nichols stayed outside? No way."

"You're right. So... Sam would leave, the better part of valor."

"Maybe."

"And Nichols bashed her head with... a heavy object. And dumped her in the pool. How's that?"

"Bad, honey. Her lungs were full of water, remember? She drowned."

"Oh. That's right."

"Good try."

"Okay, he dragged her unconscious to the pool, dumped her in, held her under until -- you know."

"Did Sam see it?"

"Of course, from his house."

"Did Nichols know that?"

"No. But he worried about it."

"Did he express those concerns to Sam?"

"Possibly... carefully."

"And mention big bucks coming in?"

"That Sam would benefit from!"

"Maybe."

"So he agreed?"

"I don't know. He could have."

Arecely spent the night, and the following morning we had a good breakfast at Coco's on Sherman Way, and parted lovingly. She was sweet when she was sweet, and I could see the wisdom of her insistence we not live together. A way to avoid volatility -- better than spending too much time with each other, vainly attempting to suppress inevitable irritations. She was smart. We each had strong wills, and opinions -- a guarantee of conflict if combined with constant association. I'd experienced that in the past, with others, including my ex.

No call from Figari the rest of the week. By then I realized we'd pay a price for stealing Sam's roll of film. Whether the photo could be used as evidence in court I didn't know. Probably learn that next semester. Of course I knew the police couldn't use illegally obtained evidence, but we weren't the police. Sam and I had not been very close over the years, but I still hated the idea of him being mixed up in this murder, if it was one. But was he mixed up in it? Figari would find out.

My next show was in Atlanta; Lionel and I would be leaving on Thursday. Some of our merchandise was shipped ahead, some we would carry with us. On Monday, Figari phoned -- he'd questioned my uncle: "A long session," he labeled it. Sam hadn't budged, yet Figari found his responses unsatisfactory. He wouldn't tell me anything more.

Arecely called him, and learned a follow-up interview was scheduled for Friday with Sam, accompanied by a lawyer, at the police station. No, we would not be allowed to attend. Just as well -- I'd be in Atlanta.

"I'm going to go over and hang out in the waiting room," she informed me later, in her apartment.

"The waiting room?"

"You know what I mean. Somewhere."

"Get Figari's permission?"

"Why should I need that? He doesn't have to talk to me if he doesn't feel like it. I'm going."

"Figari won't reveal any specifics. It's a homicide investigation!"

"Be a pessimist if you wish, hotshot, but I think your uncle will crack."

"Call me in Atlanta?" I reached over and squeezed her knee. We were in her living room on the couch.

"You'll be working." She was toying with me. I hated that. "Don't want to bother you."

"You won't bother me. Call."

"If you insist," she sighed.

"I do." She leaned her head forward, inviting me to kiss her. I did.

Of course she had another thought, which caused her to push me away. "Wait a second! Listen." She paused, thinking, and grabbed my arm. "Your uncle may have noticed his film is missing. In fact, it's likely he did. If he thought the police had it, that they knew more than they were saying, he'd spill it all, right?"

"Not a Marine."

"That's why! Honor, and all that."

"I'll concede your brilliance. But --"

"Thank you. And... he killed her."

"Why?"

"Nichols was asleep! She looks unhappy in the picture because she was telling him it was over. Get it?"

"Over?"

"Their affair, stupid. All those shots of her, his weird attitude now. He's not afraid of Nichols! He's a Marine, remember?"

"Yeah... that's right."

"Thank you. He'd watched her, he'd approached her, they'd had an affair. Maybe risky, considering the location, but she drank a lot, don't forget that. And he refused to drop it. He bashed her head the night she rejected him."

There was no denying Arecely's logic when she analyzed a legal 'fact pattern' -- her grades proved that. They were better than mine. "Okay, but it's extremely obsessive of him, to say the least."

"Don't you know how men are? They can see a woman and -- it happens. You hunt, we gather. Right?"

"Right." I thought of the girl on the airplane, Tracie.

"Some men don't know when to stop, that's all." She looked at me for confirmation.

"Right."

"That's when the law takes over."

"Alright, but you be the one to tell Figari about the pictures."

"Please, Ed. Won't you do it?"

Not only did I inform him, I took the prints and negatives in and turned them over. Figari was mad, then grateful. He developed a strategy and told me to keep out of it. I did -- I went to Atlanta with Lionel.

Just as Arecely predicted (she was psychic, no question), Sam confessed when faced with the photos. He saw the handwriting on the wall. Even his lawyer couldn't stop him.

She phoned me Friday evening, rubbing it in good:

"Men. What would you do without us?"

"Be happy?" She hung up on me.

TWO FOUNTAINS OF GRACE

Jim pressed his face into his pillow, praying the day would pass quickly. He didn't want to do what he had to do -- go to Diane, informing her her hopes were futile. But he must. Every time Jim met her she gave him that needy look, sexual, lonely, hopeless, begging him to make the move. But it wasn't in his heart. She was just a friend to him -- nothing more.

Six years earlier they'd met at work, formed an acquaintance, but Diane gradually showed signs of interest beyond that. Jim had tossed them off, believing she'd get the right idea. She didn't.

Jim, today, would set her straight at last. All this time she'd dropped hints, she'd hugged him when he didn't want to hug, she'd used that soft voice to appeal... to what? Innate sexual desire? He had none for her.

She'd be hurt, of course, when he spelled it out. She'd deny, or maybe not, that she'd harbored hopes of a more-than-friendly relationship. But he knew the truth. More often than not Jim was on the opposite side, asking women out who didn't want to go out, writing letters that went unanswered, planning ways to win someone's heart; so he knew the position she was in. Only for Jim the truth always dawned, and he'd pulled away from whichever woman showed plain lack of interest. But not Diane. She wouldn't face the facts, wouldn't let go.

Today had to be the day. No more uncomfortable lunches, phone conversations, repeated remarks like: "You're a good friend. You're like a sister to me." No, now he'd have to say it: "You seem to want more than I'm interested in offering you."

But Jim hesitated getting out of bed. He was smart enough to know that if Diane hadn't accepted reality all these years it meant she wouldn't like it now. But... it must be done.

Noon loomed ominously, the clock ticked hurriedly, the globe revolved speedily. Jim forced himself up, washed his face, ate a tasteless breakfast, dressed morosely, dreading the conversational confrontation awaiting them. She'd smile, she'd ask how he'd been, she'd hang on his words, she'd be stunned when he began the little speech. She'd refuse to acknowledge never letting go of her hope, she'd cry, she'd ask why -- the worst question.

He'd gently say he didn't feel like that toward her. She'd repeat the question: "Why?" or add a word: "Why not?" He'd tell her he didn't know, he wasn't attracted to her, can't she see that? She'd switch to a laugh and suggest they try it because how can one know if one hasn't tried it? He'd force himself to say he just did not want to. Hadn't she been able to determine that after all these years? Why did she hang on so proudly? Jim had never led her on, had even talked of other women. Why didn't she let go of it?

Probably Diane would not tell him the answer to that; she'd laugh again, and wait, but he wouldn't retreat, and she'd be angry, finally. The friendship would be damaged permanently. She'd feel belittled, crushed, put down, diminished as a human being. Jim would blame himself for not speaking up earlier. She'd drive off in her car, no hug, no cheek kiss, no soft-voiced goodbye.

He stood in his kitchen picturing all this. There was no escape. His hints had had no effect -- the truth must be boldly expressed.

One hour to go. Jim meandered into the den, sat in a chair, looked out the window. So this is the ugly spot women normally found themselves in! No big surprise they chose to not return phone calls. That had been his mistake -- seeing her over the years, calling her, having lunch,

going to movies. Just because he'd never made advances,
never been romantic, wasn't enough.

He clicked on the TV. Gene Scott, pastor to millions,
was taking communion in his studio. Jim ran to the
kitchen, fetched a small glass of wine, a piece of cracker,
and returned. Scott reminded his viewers God wanted them
to "partake worthily, discerning the Lord's body." The
wine symbolized the shed blood, "the price of redemption."
Jim drank as the pastor drank. The bread symbolized the
body offered at Calvary, the body which endured thirty-nine
stripes. "By his stripes you were healed." He ate the
cracker as the pastor ate.

"Two fountains of Grace," he'd called it. Salvation
and healing.

Jim turned off the TV. He prayed to get through the
day, to successfully tell Diane he didn't want a physical
relationship with her. It seemed simpler now.

Printed in Great Britain
by Amazon